Night

Garry Kilworth has travelled many times to the Pacific Islands and is an avid collector of myths and folk tales from the Polynesians. He has published more than fifty novels and volumes of short stories, including *The Navigator Kings* trilogy, set in the same part of the world. He has recently been elected a Fellow of the Royal Geographical Society.

Also by Garry Kilworth

Archangel
Thunderoak
Castle Storm
Wind Jammer Run
Gaslight Geezers

Nightdancer

GARRY KILWORTH

Dolphin Paperbacks

First published in Great Britain in 2002
as a Dolphin paperback
by Orion Children's Books
a division of the Orion Publishing Group Ltd
Orion House
5 Upper St Martin's Lane
London WC2H 9EA

A catalogue record for this book
is available from the British Library

ISBN 1 85881 712 9

Typeset at The Spartan Press Ltd,
Lymington, Hants

Printed and bound in Great Britain by
Clays Ltd, St Ives plc

For Clark Henstock

Arrived at the Point-of-earth,
Arrived at the Point-of-sky,
Arrived in this land, as land.
The stranger's heart is food for you.

(ritual Maori chant when passing
a magical rock or tree)

1

New Boy on the Island

John felt as if he were going to fall out of the sky. The plane was banking, turning in a large circle. There was nothing between him and a fall of a thousand metres but a thin sheet of glass. One minute the sea was beneath him, the next he was looking down on to a craggy mountain peak. He clung to the arms of the seat, afraid to close his eyes in case he felt himself hurtling through thin air. His stomach was turning over and over. Then, thankfully, the plane straightened out, and they were skimming over gullies away from that jagged volcanic rock.

'I hate it when it does that,' he said. 'Why can't they fly in straight, without turning on the side like that?'

'The pilot must know what he's doing, dear.'

'Maybe he does. Maybe he knows he's scaring me stiff, that's why he's doing it.'

His mother laughed and pointed through the window, down at the sight below.

In the middle of the small island was thick rainforest. Around the edges were the light-green waters of the lagoon. A mysterious dark-green middle, with high eerie windblown crags, sweeping down to a bright, light fringe. John could see that the people lived all around the edge of the small island, no house very far away from the dazzling white beach. Out in the lagoon, kept separate from the deep blue of the ocean by a coral reef, were small canoes with sails shaped like a crab's claw.

'How big is it?' asked John.

His mother, Mary Terangi, held his hand as they came in to land on Rarotonga, one of the Cook Islands in the Pacific Ocean.

'Oh, I'm not sure. I think it's about ten kilometres at its widest part. Not very big after New Zealand, is it?'

John stared down again as the aircraft circled the largest town, Avarua, which was not much more than a village by New Zealand standards. The island was shaped like the silhouette of an apple. There was a single road going all the way round the edge, with tracks going off towards the middle. None of them seemed to actually reach anywhere. They sort of petered out in the dense growth of trees, vines, grasses and bushes at the edges of misty-green steep cliffs.

'So this is where my ancestors came from?' said John, more to himself than his mother.

'Some of them,' his mother said, nodding.

John Terangi had mixed feelings. He felt the excitement, of course, of going to live in a place he had never seen before. But he was already missing his friends back in New Zealand. The only person he knew in this new place was his mother. She had assured him that he would soon get to know other children of his age. John wondered if there could actually be any more eleven-year-olds on such a small island.

Also his heart ached for his dog, Gip, who was now running around with a cousin on the shores of Lake Taupo. John liked his cousin, but he resented giving him his dog. Gip was a wonderful pet, full of life, always ready to go out for a run (never a walk!) and he knew several tricks. That someone else was asking him to do those tricks grieved John deeply.

There was also the question of noise and bustle.

'This place looks dead,' complained John. 'I can't see any cars on the road, let alone people . . .'

'Yes, look, there's a bus. And you won't see people from this height. We're looking down on the tops of their heads. It's like trying to see a needle from end on.'

'Well – it still looks dead. I bet there's nothing to do here. I bet I'll be bored to tears.'

'Your father came back to spend some of his childhood here, and he *loved* it.'

John's parents were Maoris, some of whose great-grandparents had come from Rarotonga. Despite being a Maori John had fair hair and blue eyes, since like many Maoris, he had European ancestors too. He was of mixed race, like a great many people in a world where travel is easy. His father was dead: killed in a car accident in Auckland. His mother was a professor of archaeology whose speciality was ancient Polynesian tools and weapons. She had been sent to Rarotonga by a museum in Auckland to excavate sites on Rarotonga and look for artefacts.

The plane landed and they disembarked. They were met outside the airport by Mr Tevete, who was the local historian. He had found them a house on the road going out of Avarua, near the church. It was a clean bungalow with a small garden. There was a grave in the garden, well kept, with a white headstone.

'My mother,' explained Mr Tevete, who owned the house. 'She'll quite like to have company. We often have family graves in our gardens here.' He smiled at John. 'My mama still likes to keep her eye on us – make sure we wipe our shoes before going into her home.'

John wasn't sure how to take that. Dead people in the garden? But true enough, looking round, he could see that other houses had similar white headstones. He must have shown concern in his expression, because

Mr Tevete suddenly said kindly, 'I'm not frightening you, am I? I don't really believe in ghosts, you know. Not walking-around ghosts, anyway. I mean she's sort of looking down from heaven.'

'That's all right,' said John. 'I'm not worried.'

But later that evening, when the sun went down as it always did in this part of the world, quickly and without any fuss, John *did* feel a little worried. The living-room window faced out to sea, with the bright beach and sparkling lagoon between. But his bedroom was at the back, and his view there was of a dark brooding inland with crags rising out of a tangle of vegetation. Everything there was folded in vines and leaves, the chaos of the growth only stopping where people with small farms kept it cut back. The jungle was like a great frozen wave of succulent plants which looked ready to wash over the houses between it and the beach.

He stared into this mass of shadows as the darkness crawled through it, wondering if anyone ever went in there at all. It seemed strange to John that here on the edge of the island was light, laughter and life, and just a few metres away an unknown world of streams and mossy rainforest floors hidden beneath dense foliage. Even though the island was only a few kilometres wide he realised that a person could get lost in the interior where natural dangers lurked.

Tucked up in an unfamiliar bed, he tried to get to

sleep, but the harder he tried the more awake he became. His head was buzzing with thoughts. Finally, at some unearthly hour, he dropped off and went into a sleep full of dreams, of falling off cliffs, of drowning in giant waves, of running through a dark forest with an unknown creature behind him. When morning came John felt thoroughly exhausted. His mother had not emerged from her room, so he went to the fridge and got himself some orange juice. Then slipping on some shorts he went out on to the veranda.

It was a bright warm morning, with a few puffs of cloud over the mountain. There were smells: of ripe fruit, waxy greenery, and a whiff of dung coming from behind the house. Out the front though, he faced the cool salt breeze from the ocean. He could see the giant ocean waves of his nightmares crashing on the reef just a few hundred metres away. They reared up until they were almost translucent green – John imagined that if you were close enough you could see the fish in them – then fell from a five-metre height down to smash on the white coral reef. The reef took all the fury out of them and only a shimmering ripple went out across the lagoon, to caress the beach in a whisper of foaming water.

'Ko 'ai to 'ou ingoa?'

John whirled round to see a boy about his own age, sitting in one of the rattan chairs at the end of the veranda.

'What?'

'Ko Mati toku ingoa.'

'Who are you?' asked John.

'I just told you, my name is Mati,' said the boy. He had a bamboo pole in his hand with a fishing line tied to the end. 'After I asked you what your name is. Don't you speak the language?'

'I only speak English,' replied John, 'and some French I learned at school.'

'You won't find much call for French here,' said Mati, grinning now. 'We don't get many French tourists. They all go to Tahiti. You should go to Tahiti with that French of yours. Everybody speaks French in Tahiti. It's the thing to do there. You could talk to anyone you liked on Tahiti. Here we speak English and our own language.'

'Look.' John tried to get control of the situation. 'What are you doing on our veranda? This is private property. My mother will be up in a minute and she'll want to know what you're doing, sitting in one of our chairs.'

'This chair?' said Mati, looking down and making no effort to get up. 'This was my gran'mam's chair. I've sat in it a million times.' He nodded at the grave. 'That's gran'mam out there. She wouldn't like you telling me off for sitting in her chair.'

'Your father is Mr Tevete?'

John's mother called from the kitchen. Apparently

she was now up and around. 'Breakfast, John. Mr Tevete's left us some lovely fruit. All sorts. Pawpaw, mangoes, melon . . .'

'Ah,' murmured Mati, 'the French boy's name is John.'

'I'm not French and you'd better go.'

But Mati didn't go. He wandered into the kitchen, following John, and introduced himself to John's mum in Cook Island's Maori. She answered him, laughing. John felt right out of it. His mother had once tried to teach him Maori, but he had resisted it, since his schoolfriends had not spoken it. It was bad enough learning French in school, without having to learn Maori at home. He listened to the pair of them chattering away before he interrupted.

'Are we going to eat breakfast?'

'Yes, yes of course, dear. Mati can stay if he likes.'

Mati liked. Then he offered to take John fishing on the reef. Now this was more like it. Fishing. There was nothing wrong with that. John changed into some old shorts and followed Mati, who found him another fishing rod. There were several kids out on the reef doing the same thing, including a girl called Sally, who spoke English with an American accent. Her mother and father came from Seattle, and had set up a hairdressing salon in Rarotonga. Sally remarked on John's fair hair, as opposed to his skin, which was darker than hers.

'You're very pretty,' she said. Sally, he had learned, was a year older than he was. 'You have lovely eyes.'

'I'm not pretty,' he said, outraged.

'All right, you're ugly then,' she said, shrugging her shoulders. 'Who cares.'

John felt a little better when he landed the biggest catch of all the group: a reddish-coloured fish, caught in one of the foaming gaps in the coral, where it had been lurking under a shelf. By the time he walked back from the reef's edge, over the coral to the white-sanded beach, he felt more at ease with the other children. Later he saw Sally in the supermarket with her mother, and in a proper dress with her short hair combed and proper shoes on her feet, she looked very grown-up. He felt shy talking to her, while his mother arranged a hair-do on the spot.

'So *you're* Professor Terangi,' said Sally's mum. 'We've been expecting you. It's a bit villagey here on the island, as you'll gather. Everyone knows everyone's business. But you get used to that. After Seattle this place is heaven. They used to call the islands "faraway heavens" didn't they, the Polynesian seafarers?'

'Yes, they did,' said Mary, smiling.

By the time evening came John felt a little more at home on the island. It wasn't Auckland, by any stretch of the imagination, but now that the unknown had become the known, he felt a little better. The kids were just kids, the same as back in New Zealand, and not creatures with the coldness of sharks. John didn't suppose for one minute he was not ever going to fall out with one or another of them, but they were ordinary just the same.

Mati – whose name John had learned meant 'March' in Maori – the month Mati had been born – had claimed John as a 'best friend' already, and was planning lots of things to do for both of them. Mati was one of those kids who liked showing the island to newcomers. And John, it had to be said, wanted to be shown. There was nothing worse than being an outsider, not knowing what the other kids meant when they said, 'Meet you outside Piri's place.' Or, 'See you in the Jam Hut.'

John had to learn the geography of the island fast, if he was to retain any credibility. He had to know where the kids went of a Saturday, of a Sunday, and after school hours. Already he knew there was no such thing as Winter, Autumn, Spring and Summer. On the island there were only the breadfruit season and the not-breadfruit season. There was so much to learn in so short a time.

At least he could swim well. All the local kids swam like fish. They had passed on knowledge of the reef: to avoid moray eels that might bite through your wading trainers; or treading on the deadly spines of the stone fish; or being attracted by the small blue-ringed octopus, also deadly; or the deadly cone shells; or being stung by sting rays, jellyfish, and other creatures of the lagoon. Sharks were not really a problem, inside the reef, but there was this host of other creatures which might be, if you were not wary, if you did not know what to look for. Once you knew, of course, the lagoon was as safe as any playground can be.

John was learning, and learning very quickly.

Tonight, he was exhausted, and fell deeply asleep, not realising that there were other predators on the island. One was out there now, in a forest closed by darkness. A savage shadow with a forgotten name, fashioned from hate and fear.

2
Shadow of the Sorcerer

There was a set of ancient stones out in the forest. They had been placed there, many centuries before, by primitive Polynesians. The people had arrived on the new island with their king, Tangiia, and the priests had laid the stones as foundations for a forest temple which became known as 'Most Sacred, Most Feared'. Young men had been sacrificed here, to earlier gods, and the earth had sucked the blood and life from their fine brave bodies. Now their bones were gripped by clay, their spirits locked to the old blocks of stone, long since covered with moss, ferns and creepers, and overshadowed by towering tropical trees with sturdy roots.

Amongst these stones lurked a presence. The Maoris would call it an evil *kabu*. Its form was not much more than a dark ragged shadow, roughly in the shape of a man.

This kabu had felt the boy's arrival on the island. It knew the boy was linked to the old people. Was he one of the Unequalled Ones, the fair-haired forest fairies who danced under the brightness of the moon? They who were known as the legendary *Tapairu*? The kabu had been seeking to grasp a fairy for five hundred years. Fairies were its natural enemies, they being creatures of virtue, while he was an engine of evil. The kabu also knew that the Tapairu had been hiding deep in the forest, keeping away from humans. But the kabu could not range far from Most Sacred, Most Feared which kept it in succour. It could not venture into the hinterland, to seek one of its ancient enemies.

To sacrifice a fairy would mean to rise again from the grave. Was this a fairy, ripe for ritual sacrifice? This fair-haired youth? The kabu's thinking was not as clear as it once had been. Centuries in the fetid dankness of the clammy leafworld rotted the minds of spirits. There was a murkiness caused by its own very gradual decay. Bitterness, fury and hate hastened its corruption. The kabu knew only that its time was running out and it needed to find a key to mortality again.

This boy appeared to be such: a descendant of the fairies.

The kabu crept towards the house. There it hovered

outside the window, looking in. The boy tossed restlessly in his bed, probably sensing the nearness of the creature who sought it. The kabu stared greedily at the object of its intentions, unable to enter a human habitation uninvited.

The kabu's weapon was a small *taiaha* spear decorated with a sorcerer's scarlet feather and tipped with a deadly poison. The kabu had to deliver this instrument of death to the boy, for it to do its evil task of killing a tapairu. At last, there was work to be done.

John woke with a start. He was drenched in sweat. A great terror gripped his mind. He didn't know what it was that had frightened him, but he knew it was full of horror. John sucked in breath, his heart racing. He stared around the room, at the moonformed shadows. One of them was moving, dancing on the wall before his eyes. There was a horrible stink coming into the room from outside the house.

'Go away!' he yelled. 'Get away from here!'

A few minutes later John's mother came into the bedroom, tying the belt of her dressing-gown.

'What is it?' she said, looking scared. 'John, whatever's the matter?'

'That thing on the wall!' He pointed.

Mary stared, then shook her head. 'It's only a palm leaf, blowing in the breeze outside the window. That's all. Just the shadow of a palm leaf. You've been having a bad dream.' She seemed to relax a little and sat on his bed, stroking his hair. 'You're all wet. You're covered in perspiration. I think it's the move that's causing all these anxiety dreams. You can come with me to the dig tomorrow. It'll give you something to focus on. Try and get to sleep now.'

'Leave the light on,' ordered John.

'Don't worry. I'll get us some drinks. Give you time to cool down. Perhaps I should have rented a place with air conditioning? I just thought those sort of houses lock out the best of a place like this – the scents of the flowers, that sort of thing.'

John managed to get through the rest of the night by snatching sleep here and there. But every so often he woke and listened hard. There was rain in the night, which hammered on the metal roof of the bungalow, and strangely enough this helped him fall into a good sleep.

When he woke and looked out of the window a thick mist was creeping around those mysterious cliffs behind the house. The atmosphere remained humid – the air hot and damp – and it was difficult to breathe. Out under the banana palms a dog was worrying some chickens. Nearby some young pigs were rooting around at the base of a pandanus tree.

Mati came and had breakfast with him again.

'This is a spooky place,' John admitted, once they were out of earshot of his mother. 'I got scared last night. I thought there was something outside the window.'

'My gran'mam,' said Mati, grinning.

'No, I'm serious,' John replied. 'Is there – is there anything in there – in those mountainous bits – the forest? You know. Are there animals? Monkeys? Wild-cats? Anything like that?'

Mati saw that John was quite frightened and resisted the temptation to impress him with fabled monsters.

'No. No animals. When our ancestors arrived here there were only birds. Now we have a few things like pigs, dogs and rats. You probably heard a pig snuffling. They often scare me when I'm not expecting one. That's what it was, I bet.'

John did not think that what he heard was a pig, but he let the subject drop.

Mati asked, 'What's your mum doing here?'

'Here on the island? She's come to do some digs. You know, excavations? She wants to find out about the old people.'

'The old people? They used to eat missionaries. Is she looking for the bones of missionaries?'

John realised he was being made fun of. He gave Mati a wry look.

'No, of course not. She's looking for weapons and tools. That's her speciality. She wants to find things to take back to New Zealand for the museums there. And for the museum on the island.'

'What sort of things?'

John was familiar with many of the artefacts his mother had already found, simply because they lay around the house until she delivered them to the museums. Weapons were quite exciting to a young boy. If she had been collecting woven mats or necklaces he would not have been quite so interested.

'Spears and clubs, that sort of thing. But if she finds anything else – pots or musical instruments – she'll get those too. Like shell trumpets and wooden flutes. Last year she found a *pu kaea* near Christchurch. That's a wooden trumpet.'

Mati said scornfully, 'I know what *pu kaea* is,' but it was evident to John that he didn't. There was some sort of loss of pride in being told something in *the language* by someone who didn't even speak it. Mati clearly felt his honour was at stake.

'Do you want to come to the dig?' John asked. 'Mum's going to take me today. You can come if you want.'

'I don't mind,' Mati said, shrugging. 'Sally will want to come too – she always does.'

John didn't mind that and asked his mother.

'If you all stay out of my way, I don't mind who comes. On second thoughts, yes I do. I don't want every child from the town traipsing up there with us. Just the three of you then. We're going to Needle Rock. There's an overhang just beyond it where I'm told there's a likelihood of finding some remains.'

'Needle Rock?' said Mati, once informed. 'Of course I know it. Everyone knows the Needle.'

The path to this natural monolith ran up from behind the town, into brushland first of all, then finally into the rainforest proper. When they set out there was a party of seven: four adults and the three children. The track was well worn. It went past the Needle, which stood like a roughly hewn cathedral spire on a high ridge, and down into the valleys below, eventually leading right the way across the island's interior. So far as Mati knew it was the only track across the middle of Rarotonga.

'We ought to use it, one day,' suggested Sally. 'I've never been across the island. Have you Mati?'

'Course I have,' snorted Mati, in the same scornful way that he had 'known' what a *pu kaea* was.

'We'll have to take a compass, map and water. That sort of thing,' said John. 'A proper expedition. Who's going to be the leader?'

'Me. This is my island,' said Mati. 'You two are visitors.'

It was Sally's turn to snort. '*Your* island! You don't own it. I've lived here for two years – and I'm the oldest. I should be the leader, being the oldest.'

It was on the tongues of both boys to protest that she was a *girl* and therefore ineligible, but some inner voices wisely told them that this was not a sensible argument, especially since John's mother was a woman and was leading the excavation group. In any case, neither youth was able to stand up to Sally in an argument. She was a girl in age and body, but like many girls of her age was almost a woman in intellect. Sally could tear strips off them in any verbal exchange, then hang those strips out to dry in the sun like victory banners.

John realised he had the weakest position of all and that all he would get was casting vote for one of the other two.

'Who can read maps?' he asked.

'That doesn't matter,' said Mati, taking up the lead on the rainforest path and establishing a sort of psychological advantage. 'There's no good maps anyway. It's local knowledge that's needed. I've been across already.'

'You're a big liar,' said Sally, bluntly.

Instead of getting mad, Mati turned and grinned. 'You're just a year older than the both of us. How's that going to help?'

John quickly intervened, before Sally exploded.

'Look, why don't you toss a coin?'

They agreed to this, since neither Mati nor Sally had any good reason for being the leader of an expedition.

Sally won. John was pleased about that, because he felt if Mati had won it would still have remained unsettled from Sally's point of view. None of them would have heard the last of it until they had actually got across the island, and perhaps not even then.

When they reached the site of the dig, the children could not actually get down to the spot where the excavations had to take place. There were four men and a woman with Mary. There were two local workmen, a civil servant and two people on the staff of the Cook Islands' Museum. The spot where the digging would start was down a sheer escarpment, about ten metres below the ridge, with an ever steeper drop beyond the ledge. The children could see some moss-covered rocks on the ledge, but that was all. It was, John agreed, pretty boring.

After watching the workmen build some rickety steps down the slope, the children agreed to go back to town.

'We want to go swimming,' said John to his mother.

Mary was preoccupied, but she gave this her attention.

'Where?'

'In the lagoon.'

'Well, be very, very careful. You don't know these waters.'

Mati said, 'I do. I'll look after him.'

Mary agreed to this and the three young people went back down the path. John was taking up the rear, with Sally in front and Mati in the middle. Sally and Mati were discussing the expedition, when John felt something cold touch the back of his neck. They were in thick brush at this point, with lots of tall overhanging saplings bearing creepers.

He slapped at his neck the way one would do with a mosquito bite, and whirled round.

For a moment he just stood there, staring back along the shaded path, into the leafy undergrowth behind.

It was almost as if someone had blown breath on his neck – icy breath. Was there anyone there? The path was freckled with shadow as the bright sunlight struggled to get through the lacework of leaves. There was movement, but it seemed only from the breeze-blown foliage.

'Hey!' he said, weakly.

No one answered. When he turned back, he found that Sally and Mati were nowhere to be seen. They had not missed him, and were obviously much further along the winding path, shrouded by tall, spiky clumps of bamboo and tropical grasses.

John was alone in this strange landscape. Suddenly a dark shape seemed to detach itself from the mottled, speckled shadows. It flew at John's face.

3
An Expedition into the Rainforest

'Hey!' yelled John, in fright. 'Go away!'

The shape veered off, out away from the bushes and trees, into the sunlight. It was a large bird. A predator by the look of it. Some kind of buzzard or falcon with a wide wingspan. It spiralled up, into the blinding sun, out of John's vision.

Mati and Sally came running back.

'What's the matter?' cried Sally.

John, still a little shaken, pointed. 'There was a big bird – I don't know – it flew straight at me.'

Mati said, 'That's 'cause you're standing in the only opening to this glade. It couldn't fly up. It'd get its wings tangled in the branches. You've got the frights, you have. What kind of bird was it?'

'I dunno.' John was a little rattled by Mati's tone. 'I'm new here.' He added after a moment, 'Some kind of raptor, I think.'

'Probably a white-bellied sea-eagle,' sniffed Sally.

'What, in the forest?' Mati said. 'It was probably somethin' smaller really, like a frigate bird.'

'It doesn't matter what it was,' said an exasperated John. 'It scared the pants off me. Let's get out of here.'

Later in the day they explained to their various parents that they wanted to cross the island. An expedition. Mati's mum came to see John's mum. Mati's mum said she thought it would be all right if they had an adult with them.

'They can camp out overnight,' she said. 'We did that when we were children. It's very exciting, camping in the jungle.'

'They can't come to much harm, can they?'

'Not with an adult looking after them. My sister Manea will do it. She's into girl guiding and that sort of thing. She works at the Anani Backpackers Hostel. I'll ask her.'

'You sure she wouldn't mind?' said Mary.

'Mind? She'd love it.'

Manea did indeed show great enthusiasm for the expedition. Manea was about thirty years of age and one of those women who preferred to remain an aunt rather than become a mother herself. She loved children round her (she said) but not all the time. She also loved dancing and athletics and swimming and fishing and barbecues and beach volley ball and just about everything outdoors in life. Hiking was not her speciality, that being the hula, but it came in her top ten activities. Camping out overnight was in there somewhere too.

'We'll have a great time,' she told the three would-be walkers, 'so long as you do what you're told and don't stray from the path. It doesn't look it, but it's easy to get lost in there. The undergrowth grows very fast and if the track hasn't been used for a time, it'll be hard to see.'

Those words were to ring in John's ears, later.

John was gradually beginning to adjust to life on the island. He still missed Gip, and the wide open spaces of New Zealand, but things on Rarotonga were not as bad as he first imagined. He no longer felt as if he were locked in a wardrobe. There *was* space to walk, space to breathe. It was certainly a colourful place, with many exotic birds and many more exotic fish in the lagoon. If you wanted all things bright and beautiful, Rarotonga was the place to get it. The people were mostly friendly, with only one or two grumps, but those you could get anywhere. John had started school now and though he had expected a rough first week or two – kids can freeze one another out – he had not been picked on especially and stories of his former life in New Zealand were in demand.

'Have you seen *Once We Were Warriors?*' said one boy to him. 'All about the Maoris in New Zealand?'

'It's *Once Were Warriors,*' replied John. He hadn't seen it. It was rated 18 and over, but without actually saying so he managed to convey that he had seen it. He knew enough about the film, which had been widely talked about in New Zealand, to give a good account of the plot, and he had seen the main male actor, Temuera Morrison, in a television soap. 'It was brilliant. A bit violent, but who cares?'

'Oh, yeah,' the kid nodded back, 'who cares?'

John felt a bit ashamed of his pretence, but being a 'new kid' he was a little desperate to be accepted as quickly as possible. No one knew him here, properly. They didn't know how good he was at cricket or how bad at mathematics. They didn't know he had cycled from New Plymouth to Wanganui – some 100 kilometres – and had come in sixth in his age group out of two hundred cyclists. They didn't know that he had once broken a friend's toy train on purpose because he had been jealous. They didn't know he had found a lady's purse containing seventeen dollars and had handed it in to the police without a second thought. They didn't know whether he was devil or angel, or a mixture of both.

He *wanted* them to know him. He wanted them to

understand him and his short history. He did not like being a mystery.

Back in the house, when he was on his own, he did a lot of reading. He enjoyed stories by the New Zealand writer Margaret Mahy, such as *The Haunting*. And others. Comics too. He would lie on the crisp white sheets of his bed in the hot afternoon and devour comics by the dozen, swapping them with Mati and others for those he had not read.

One of his favourite occupations was lying under the mosquito net with a tray of ice cubes by his side and a *Sandman* comic. He would pop ice cubes into his mouth with his right hand and crunch through them like sweets, flicking the pages of the comic over with his left hand which remained dry. In the background would be the sound of the ocean waves booming along the coral reef, and the many noises of the wildlife. If he glanced up he could see the dazzling white walls of the nearby church, to which the ladies wore their beautiful magnolia-hued paper hats on a Sunday, and from which issued such a wonderful rich sound of bass, tenor and soprano voices, you would think a world-class choir was within.

If it was night, the beat of the log drums – often fast and furious – would enter through his window and he knew that somewhere on the island swivel-hipped women and lithe men were swathed in blooms and grass kilts and were dancing the hula.

It was not the worst place in the world to live.

On the weekend set for the trek, Manea led her small party over the ridge past the Needle, and down the other side into the rainforest. It was a hot, sultry morning, destined to get hotter. The three children had packs on their backs and carried plenty of water. John had his Swiss Army knife, with all its pocket tools: a chance at last to use it for something other than sharpening pencils. Mati had a monocular, given to him by his grandfather, which Sally insisted on calling a telescope. Sally herself was wearing a tan baseball cap making her lean face look different and bringing on the shyness the two boys felt towards older girls. It wasn't so bad when she looked like ordinary Sally, but when she changed into this young woman with a keen look it confused them.

'Right, you lot,' said Manea, as they battled down through the creepers and vines, into the muddy heart of the island, where streams criss-crossed each other falling from the misty heights of the mountain. 'While we're walking along, I'll tell you about the old gods, the ancient ones, who used to look after us before Christianity . . .'

'Like *Tiki*,' said Mati, anxious to establish his birthright place on the island.

'Well, yes, but Tiki wasn't actually a god, he was our first ancestor, like Adam in the Bible. That's why we had his image on our canoes. He can see things past, present and future. He'll see storms coming before we do. Squalls created by the great Maori sea-god, *Tangaroa* and the wind-god *Hanui-o-Rangi*. Or perhaps terrible storms of thunder and lightning made by the thunder-god *Tawhaki* whose mate *Uira*, the lightning, flashes out of his armpits as he strides across the world . . .'

Manea went on in this vein, explaining the old gods to the children, who only half-listened, telling folklore stories about the demi-god trickster *Maui*, to which they paid more attention, since in Oceania, the world of the Pacific Ocean, Maui is as well known to every man, woman and child as is Puck to mortals of Western isles.

Maui is a shapechanger, a mischievous sprite, a powerful magician, a devious genius. Maui wears a thousand faces and every one of them his own. Maui wears another thousand faces belonging to others. He is wonderful and he is terrible. Maui fished New Zealand from the bottom of the sea, he stole fire from the witch his grandmother, he grew the first coconut. Maui can be a fowl, a fish, a fern. He can be a rat, dog or pig. Once, he changed heads with his wife while walking along, to fool some villagers. Once he defeated *Te Tuna* the Monster Eel, by entering his body and swelling, thus rending Te Tuna apart.

During the walk, John took up the rear of the line.

He was anxious not to pick up leeches. Schoolfriends had told him that the blood-suckers were to be found sticking to the underside of moist leaves. He hoped that the others, walking ahead, would brush the plants aside for him to pass untouched. It didn't quite work out that way – the fronds had a habit of springing back and lashing him – but when he found that nothing stuck to him after several of these whippings he stopped worrying.

They walked all day, not seeing very much but plants, but feeling rather proud of themselves.

Towards evening, Sally said, 'What about here, Manea? In this glade. Look, there's a stream over there where we can get washing water. And I can feel a breeze from the sea.'

'That's because we're quite high up at this point,' said Manea. 'Yes, this is as good a place as any.'

Manea took off her backpack, larger than that of the others, and began to unpack it. John was concerned to see that she had brought no tent with her. He said so.

'Tent?' Manea laughed. 'We don't need any tents. We'll make some bivouacs out of saplings and palm leaves, and any pandanas leaves we can find, though those are getting rare now. You'll see how good they are for keeping off the rain. You think the first people on this island came with tents? All they had were themselves and some tools . . .'

None of the three children relished the thought of

sleeping on the ground under leaf thatch. There were ants everywhere, and other insects, some of them quite large. And there was still the thought of leeches in their minds. However, they got on with the tasks set them by Manea and found themselves enjoying the art of creating a campsite. Once it was done and the ground sheets laid in the bivouacs, they didn't feel quite so alienated from their surroundings.

Shadows crept away. The green and grey crags of the mountain seemed to swell and dominate. They took on a form of life, as if they were waiting for something. Then darkness fell, obliterating everything. Around the camp fire, Manea told them more stories of fairies and monsters. Tales of the *Lipsipsip* – dwarves who lived in ancient trees and rocks; of the *Ponaturi* – vicious sea fairies who ripped people apart and ate their arms and legs; of the *Tapairu* – that ancient race of fairies who loved to dance under the full moon.

One of the 'monsters' which fascinated John was called *Ulupoka*, and he was a minor god who had been beheaded in a battle. He had lost his body and now his head was supposed to roam the earth, being blown along island beaches by the wind, his long hair leaving flail marks in the sand. If Ulupoka bit your foot in the night, you would die by morning, so it was best not to let your feet poke out of the ends of the bedblankets, to avoid such a thing happening.

'Where do all these stories come from?' asked John. 'Who makes them up?'

Manea said, 'No one knows how myths come about. Or where folk tales come from. They just seem to gather themselves together and gradually work themselves into existence. I think there's *some* truth in them, somewhere.'

Sally scoffed. 'Oh, no – not the head of a giant god, rolling along the beaches. You *can't* believe that's true.'

'No, not exactly. But they exist in our *minds*. In that part of us which needs another world, a stranger world, where magic is possible and things are never quite what they seem.'

'Well I don't believe any of it,' said John, his own heartbeat telling him he was lying. 'Not a word. I'm going to bed.'

He went to one of the two bivouacs, where he and Mati were sleeping, and crawled into his sleeping-bag. Once wrapped like a cocoon he felt more secure. The bugs and forest floor life had been forgotten. His mind was full of supernatural creatures now. They roamed around his consciousness like dinosaurs once roamed the earth.

A few minutes later Mati came into the bivouac and got into his own sleeping-bag. The two of them lay there, staring up at their leafy ceiling, thinking their own thoughts, then one after the other, they fell asleep with the noises of the jungle all around them.

Like the waves of the sea falling on the reef, these were pleasant, lulling sounds. There was nothing disturbing in the music of crickets and their kind.

John woke suddenly, later in the night. A bright moon was glowing through the network of branches. Lacework shadows rippled on their camping ground. Somewhere near, water was trickling over bamboo. A bird screeched in the stillness.

John felt very thirsty. He rose and went outside, looking for the water containers. Finding one hanging from a branch, he took a long drink. Then he stared about him. It was all very strange. Very strange. He had never felt like this before, anywhere. There was an air of expectancy about the place. Was it him? Was he supposed to do something? Say something? It was all very vague, very misty in his mind.

Then he heard it.

A small voice, calling his name, from the undergrowth.

'Boy. Boy.'

He was quite calm. His heart was steady.

'Boy. Come.'

Someone wanted him.

John walked into the dense, leafy darkness which surrounded the glow from the embers of the fire.

4

Dancing with the Fairies

The voice was beguiling, enticing. As if in a deep dream, John followed the sound. It led him along a rainforest path no wider than a goat track. The words *Boy, follow* being used as a lure, called softly through the fronds of the plants, and John eventually found himself in a glade with a rock overhang and a thin waterfall dropping into a clear pool. It was a beautiful place: green, with soft turf underfoot and wild flowers hanging over a mossy bank, dipping their heads in the water. Around the open grassy area was a ring of hibiscus shrubs. John thought it strange that the blooms of these bushes were open, even though it was night.

The soft moonlight fell on thirty to forty people standing in the glade. They were people with fair hair that fell down their shoulders and backs. Of average height and stature they appeared delicate-boned. When they moved to greet him, they were light on their feet. There was a kind of fire in their footsteps. Their eyes shone as if they were fashioned from silver and their tiny white teeth flashed brilliant smiles.

Yet John sensed a frightening strangeness about them. Instinctively he knew they were not mortal. There was that in their quick supple movements, in their general demeanour, which warned him that these creatures did not have human ways or feelings, did not think or react to things in the same manner as he did. They had their own way, he was sure. They were not to be trusted: not because they were untrustworthy, but because they had a different code of ethics, a different set of morals from human beings. They had a different idea of right and wrong.

'Come, boy,' said one. 'Come and dance.'

It was as if these words were a signal. All at once musicians began to play: reed pipes, drums, flutes. The music was fast and furious. The creatures began to dance – and how they danced! In grass kilts and bedecked with flowers they leapt and jumped and twirled and turned, as if trying to spin golden garments from the shafts of moonlight hitting the glade. John felt his hand being grasped. He was pulled into the grass glade. There he was urged to 'dance!' by the person who had called him from his sleep and led him into the midst of magic.

'Dance!' said the creature.

John stood and stared. Looking around him at first he could not tell male from female. They all looked pretty. They all moved with such electric grace. Their forms were sinuous and serpentine. They were beings created for pure joy, from pure delight. Their hair flailed the air, swishing past John's face, as they whirled on their toes.

'I can't do this,' he said, looking at the complicated steps, the gymnastic movements of his fellow dancers. 'I'm just an ordinary boy.'

Yet, the music seemed both bizarre *and* familiar, both at the same time. It chilled his conscious mind with its antique eeriness, yet in the far recesses of his subconscious there awakened a response to something he knew. He *had* heard this sound before, somewhere, way back in the ancient days of the island.

But surely that was silly? John had not been alive then. He knew nothing about those years.

Yet the music was insistent. It knew him. He knew it. Somehow. Sometime. Somewhere.

All of a sudden he found himself leaping furiously with the others around him, matching their twists and turns, their tricky flashing dance steps.

'Hey, look at me!' he cried, the joy flooding into his

heart, surging through his body. 'I can dance. I can do it.'

He copied them. He imitated every movement he saw, no matter how complicated. And when he had done something once, he was able to repeat it, without recourse to the originator. All at once he found himself inventing his own steps, his own movements. Others began to copy *him.* They laughed in glee. There was not a glum face to be seen in the whole glade. Everyone was happy. Everyone was dancing.

Occasionally John had to stop, drink from the clear pool, before flinging himself back into the fray. There was no time to think, no time to stand and stare, only to dance. His fellow dancers did not even pause for refreshment. They danced non-stop, as the moon moved slowly across the sky, its beams now illuminating an old stone, now a tree with buttress roots, now a large bright spider's web, knitting together the branches. The stars also travelled their courses across the night sky, like jewelled cockroaches crawling around the dome of heaven. Flinging his head back while he danced, John found he recognised the names of constellations.

There was *Kaavei* 'Octopus Tentacle'. There was *Matariki,* 'Small Face'. And *Te Rakau Tapu* 'The Sacred Timber'. Many more names. Not the names John's European ancestors had used – Aries, Pleiades, Alpha Centauri – but the star names used by the ancient navigators who had found Rarotonga, and had settled here.

What's happening to me? John thought, one part of him alarmed at his hidden knowledge. Am I still dreaming? Shall I wake up in a minute and find myself in a great sweat of fear? But he did not feel afraid. He felt exalted. He felt wonderful.

Just before dawn the music stopped. Suddenly. At the blink of an eye. The dancers stopped too, fell where they stood. They lay on the turf and stared up at the greying sky. It seemed as if the fading stars were being blown away by a morning breeze. The moon had turned to the colour of pale cheese. Huge fruit bats floated silently on drumskin wings between palms. Birds began to sing. Spiders as large as John's hand scuttled for the shade of large waxy leaves, their eyes no longer like bright tiny lights as they had been in moonshine. Cicadas rattled their legs against their bodies, preparing for the day's concert.

A conch-shell trumpet sounded somewhere a long way away. The sound floated over the canopy of the rainforest. In an instant the dancers had vanished, not a trace of them left behind.

John fell into an exhausted sleep, by the pool.

When he woke, befuddled and hot, it was some time in the afternoon. Insects buzzed around his head, settling on his face and drinking his perspiration. Splashing cool water on his face from the waterfall he tried to collect his thoughts. What had happened? Oh, yes, the dancing. And where were they now, those light-footed creatures? Nowhere to be seen, that was for sure. But John thought their village must be close by. He recalled thinking them supernatural creatures, but surely that was his night brain at work? Surely it was the moonlight and the balmy evening air – the dreamlike atmosphere of past-midnight in the middle of the rainforest – which had played on his brain?

'They're real people,' he said to himself. 'They have to be.'

He tried to find the path back to the campsite where Manea, Mati and Sally were presumably fretting over his absence. He realised he was probably giving them a great fright. Manea especially would be worried, being responsible for the whole group.

But the tracks seemed all overgrown with foliage. He could find no clear path back through the rainforest which was not spiked with thorn bushes, or entangled with creepers and vines.

The next thing he attempted was to find the village where the fair-haired people lived. That too proved to be impossible. He could not even find the glade again. He found himself wandering in the half-darkness of the rainforest: tall trees and their attendant plants –

ferns that grew from their trunks a hundred feet up – blocked out the sunlight. All the while he was accompanied by the droning of insects: the buzz-saw sound of cicadas that made his ears ring and dulled his thinking.

Before he knew it, the evening was coming on again.

He had no compass with him. No maps. He could only guess by the sun which way to walk. So long as he did not go in circles, he told himself, he would eventually burst through the jungle *somewhere* on the island. John tried stopping every so often and listening, hoping to hear the sound of the sea breaking on the reef, but even when the cicadas ceased for the day, the night crickets took over.

John was lost. Thoroughly lost. He knew the best thing for him to do now was seek high ground, where he could climb a tree and find a viewpoint. But the escarpments he came across were vertical jagged places, frightening in their steepness. There was no way he could climb up to such heights without risk of falling. And if he fell in the rainforest, the dense dark rainforest, and broke a bone in his leg or body, he might die before he was found. He dare not even twist an ankle.

Later, as darkness fell, John gave up walking and eventually found a place to sleep: a soft mossy bank by a stream. There was cloud cover, blocking the moon: no forest dancers. No dancing.

*

The boy was out of reach.

The child was deep in the rainforest, under the protection of the tree gods and stone gods, which filled the interior.

That the child was a tapairu, an Unequalled One, descendant of that ancient fairy race, was no longer in question. He had danced with them, under the bright moon. His feet had burned with the lightness of fire. The child had fairy in his blood, in his soul, in his far past.

One or two mortals had married fairies. Their off-spring had sometimes stayed with the fairies, but in one or two cases had walked out of the rainforest and taken up life as a human. The boy was obviously a descendant of one of those who had preferred human company.

Frustration filled the kabu's shadowy, flimsy form. He wanted to grasp the fairy-child by its fair hair and drag it to Most Sacred, Most Feared. Once there the kabu could influence the boy: appear before it as a shade of human form, indistinguishable from a real man. If the boy could be led to the bamboo trap which contained the small but deadly ritual spear, the sacrifice could then take place. The God of Sorcerers would then grant the kabu's body resurrection.

To live again in human form!

That was the goal, the ultimate desire.

Yet it could not happen until the boy was in his grasp.

The kabu moaned, his voice floating out over the rainforest canopy like the sound of a conch trumpet.

Creatures like this one, from the world of shadows, are almost eternally in despair. It is their anguish, their utter misery, which keeps them from disappearing altogether. You could say they were formed of such feelings. Darkness of the soul is a terrible thing to suffer, even for a long-dead sorcerer with evil intentions. His shadow-heart was like a twisted rag, knotted so hard it had become a rope. His shadow-mind was a confused maze of unfulfilled questions. His shadow-eyes saw nothing but death and the rot after death. He was like some forgotten thing without hope, left to fester and grow only in corruption.

Yet, he did have hope!

The boy would have to come out of the rainforest at some time. This fairy-child would soon fall into the kabu's clutches. In the meantime the kabu could prepare.

Since the kabu could not capture the boy himself, his shadow-form being too frail, he would have to make a creature more substantial than himself. A creature which could attack the boy, render him helpless, so that the kabu could then deal the blow of death. Perhaps a *Vis*, a Polynesian vampire? Or a *Balepa*, a corpse still wrapped in its burial mat, which floated through the air? Finally the kabu decided upon a *puata*.

Yes, the puata would do very well.

5

Boy with the Magic Feet

The night passed without incident. John had bad dreams, but none that woke him screaming. Nor did he 'sleepwalk' again, as he had done the night before. He guessed he was far from the village of the fair-haired people and that their dancing drums were beyond his earshot.

In the morning John's thirst began to rage. He drank from streams. In any other place but a Pacific island this might have been very dangerous, but fortunately the Rarotongan interior had no animals to pollute the water. In New Zealand, with thousands of sheep around, he would have been in real trouble.

He walked and walked. His clothes became en-grimed with sweat and dirt. Twigs entangled themselves in his hair. Burrs stuck to his shorts and shirt. By the time he came to a huge pipeline, he looked like something out of nature, a boy of leaves and grass.

The pipeline seemed to cross the island. Climbing a tree, he was able to stand on top of this pipe. John had always had a good sense of balance. He walked along it knowing that at last he was going to find his way out.

When he reached the edge of the rainforest and could see the sea for the first time in two days, he sobbed in relief. Wearily he climbed down from the pipe and made his way to the road. One or two cars passed him, but failed to recognise his distress. Then he managed to stop the next round-the-island bus, persuaded the driver to take him on board with a promise of later payment, and eventually reached home.

Mary was out with search parties, frantically looking for him. When she was found and the search parties recalled, she came home and grasped John tightly, making him feel uncomfortable.

'Are you all right? Are you hurt?'

'No – no, not hurt. I'm fine, Mum.'

Mary seemed to be fighting anger amongst her other emotions.

'What happened? Did they lose you?'

'I don't know. No, Manea didn't lose me. I lost myself. I don't know how it happened. I walked in my sleep.'

'You what?' Mary's tone was incredulous.

'I – I just found myself walking at night. I don't know why. It just happened. Then I met these people and we danced . . .'

'You danced.' Mary's tone was now flat, a sign of her increasing incredulity.

'Yes. I know it sounds stupid, but that's what happened. It was like some kind of dream. I just found myself dancing with these people. Then they disappeared somewhere and I couldn't find their village.'

Mary said, carefully, 'John, there are no people in the middle of the island.'

'There are,' he said, stoutly, 'I danced with them.'

She shook her head. 'Maybe it was a party? Maybe some of the islanders gathered together and went in there for a party? I'll ask around. Nothing else happened to you, though. You – you weren't – molested in any way?'

John felt shocked. 'No. Of course not.'

'Not "of course not" – these things happen. You should know that not everyone on the earth is to be trusted, John. I don't know who these people were – do you? Did they say?'

'They just danced,' John answered, miserably.

'If they were so trustworthy, they'd have taken you back to the coast with them. I can't think why they were so irresponsible. Even if they were drunk or something. They could surely see you're just a young boy. Were they drinking hard? Well, I'll make some enquiries. In the meantime,' she gave him a hug, 'don't scare me like that again.' She was suddenly crying. 'It was horrible. I don't know when I've ever been so frightened.'

Fortunately Sally and Mati arrived. Mary went into the kitchen to finish her weeping alone. The two children looked at John with some awe.

'What was it like? Being lost?' asked Mati. 'Were you scared?'

'Not all the time,' admitted John. 'But I did get thirsty. I had to drink from a stream.'

'I want the doctor to check you out!' yelled Mary, from the kitchen, making John wince.

'You should be all right,' said Sally. 'My uncle came to stay and he insisted on drinking from a waterfall. He didn't get sick.'

'Well, anyway,' John said, 'I feel tired. I'm sorry I spoiled the expedition. I didn't do it on purpose.'

When he went to school, John found he was a bit of a hero. It's a strange thing, but if something stupid results in a dangerous adventure, other kids are envious. John felt a bit of a fraud as other kids asked him what happened, how he managed to stay alive in the jungle. Some of the children were so excited they spoke to him in Polynesian and he had to tell them he didn't understand. They didn't mind. They simply asked him the same questions again, but this time in English.

He vowed then to begin learning a few words of the local language. John didn't like the fact that others could talk around him and he was ignorant of what they were saying.

When he went home that evening, his mother had some things to say to him.

'I don't think you could have met anyone in the rainforest, John.'

'I wasn't lying,' he said, firmly. 'I've got no reason to tell lies. I saw these people. I danced with them.'

'Perhaps you were thirstier than you thought? Maybe you were a little feverish. Those were probably hallucinations.'

'I'm just telling you what happened.'

Mary sighed. 'Well, there were no parties. I've checked all over. Anyway, people tell me they wouldn't go that deep into the rainforest, just to have a party. I think we'll have to draw a line under the dancing.'

'I must have been doing something all night. I was so tired in the morning I didn't wake up.'

'Maybe it was just the walking that exhausted you?'

They said no more about it. John had a check-up at the doctor's, just to make sure he had not suffered heat exhaustion, which is very dangerous. As for the water, he seemed to have suffered no ill-effects and Mary thought it best to draw a line under that too. She kept a good eye on him over the next few days, but when John showed no signs of fever or headaches, she allowed herself to forget the incident.

Three weeks after the expedition, there was a night of entertainment and hula dancing in the courtyard of one of the local beach taverns. There was entertainment for the children. John was taken by Mary, and Mati was there with his mum and dad. Sally too.

The first act of the evening was fire-walking. Three men from another island baked stones in a fire until they were white-hot, then skipped over them as if they were stepping stones in a stream. John could see the vapour rise from their feet, as their soles touched the hot stones. He wondered how they could shut their minds to the pain that must have been shooting up through the bottom of their feet. But they showed no sign of being uncomfortable in any way. Someone threw a glass of drink on one of the stones, to test its hotness, and the liquid sizzled.

Then a group from Aitutaki Island, another of the Cook Islands, sang some of the old songs in Polynesian. John had to watch Mati and the others to see when to laugh and when to cry. He was picking up one or two words now, but not yet enough to understand a whole song. He knew enough to cry out *'Meitaki ma'ata!'* ('Very good!') when the soloist had finished a particularly good rendering of a sung tale about the founding of Aitutaki. Mati told John and Sally that the singer was a descendant of the original 'Speaker in the Seventh Canoe' in the seagoing fleet that first landed on the island. The story of that discovering voyage to the island and how it was found had been passed down to him by his forebears.

All the while the chefs had been roasting meats on the barbecue. By the time the singer had finished the meal was ready. The children took their paper plates full of meat and salad to eat on the beach. The night was soft and the waves were gently plashing on the sea strand. All around them were thousands of square miles of ocean embedded with jewel-like islands such as the one on which they lived. Moonlight flickered on the deep-sea waves beyond the reef, and the placid lagoon, which tamed those waves, shone like an emerald under the mellow beams.

Large countries and continents could go roaring forth, racing like mighty engines, while islands such as this rolled forward in a smooth and timeless way, beating to the rhythm of the tides and currents of the great sea moving around its coral heart.

'I love it here,' said Sally, sighing. 'Seattle was so noisy.'

'It's noisy here,' pointed out John. 'Listen to the crickets back there in the mangroves!'

'Different kind of noise though, surely,' said Mati, who had been once to Auckland. 'I don't even hear the crickets. Nor the waves. Only my old gran'mam calling me from the garden. *Mati*, she says. *Mati my grandson, there's a stranger in the house stealin' all your lovely mango jam what I made you before I left.*

Sally laughed, knowing that Mati's dad had sent three jars of jam around to the bungalow.

John didn't take the bait. Instead he bit into a chicken leg, ignoring Mati's attempts to tease him.

While the children were eating a drummer started to beat out a rapid rhythm on the log drums. It was time for the hula. A young woman of around eighteen years of age was standing in lamplight. She started swaying from side to side, smoothly and swiftly, keeping time to the drummer's beat.

John's eyes glazed over on hearing the sound. He slowly put his chicken bone on the side of his plate, then put the plate on the sand. Then he leapt to his feet and began dancing, furiously, kicking sand this way and that, into the food on the plates of the other two. In his mind he was back with the people in the middle of the island.

'Hey!' yelled Mati. 'That's not funny.' He looked at Sally, expecting her to remonstrate too, but Sally's attention was on John. She stared in amazement at him as his feet danced faster and faster, keeping up with the increasing pace of the drummer.

'John!' she said, alarmed. 'What's the matter.'

But John was lost in the music in his head. He could hear nothing outside the rattle and thrump of drumsticks on hollow wood. His face was pure concentration as his feet flew and his hips twisted.

Beach crabs, disturbed by the thumping on the ground over their sand tunnels, came up on the tips of their legs to see what was going on, their stalk eyes poking out of their holes.

Mati now stared in wonder too. For it was clear that John was a very good hula dancer. Brilliant in fact. Mati felt a tinge of envy at the skill John was demonstrating. All islanders aspire to become the best dancers in their district. And here was John, only a few weeks on the place, outdancing every boy Mati knew. John could have won competitions involving *all* the Cook Islands, and there were some pretty good dancers on those small remote groups, there being little else to do there but eat, sleep, fish and dance the night away.

'Where did you learn to do that?' asked Mati indignantly, thinking John had been holding back on him.

But John appeared not to have heard. The perspiration was pouring from his brow. He was lost in a world of rhythm. Only when the drummer stopped, at the end of the woman's dance, did John cease dancing. Then he simply stared out to sea for a few minutes, seemingly coming down to earth, before sitting down.

Sally dumbly sat down too.

Mati said, 'Hey, don't you answer a person?'

'What?' asked John, genuinely puzzled. 'What's the matter?'

'You ignored me.'

'Oh – did I? I couldn't have heard. What did you say?'

'I said, where did you learn to dance like that?'

John shook his head as if he didn't know what his friend was talking about. 'Dance like what?'

6
Walking in Dreams

John was lying in bed with the wind whispering in the palms outside. Through the window he could see the mountains, their dark crags breaking up the moonlit night sky. He had been staring at this scene for more than an hour, ever since he had seen a corpse floating on a rush mat pass by the window, wrapped in burial rags. It had called his name.

'Boy. Boy. Follow me. I will lead you to a place where there are war helmets richly decorated with red feathers and cloaks made of the finest white dogskin.'

Strangely, John had not been afraid, even though he knew dead people should not float past his window and talk to him. It seemed perfectly natural, like the sound of the waves on the shore, or the wind in the trees.

The reason John had not leapt out of bed and

followed the talking corpse was because he had no interest in helmets covered in red feathers, nor in cloaks of dogskin. John was unaware that to an ancient Polynesian such things were wealth. Red feathers were as diamonds to those old people and dogskin cloaks as ermine gowns. The kabu, the sorcerer's shadow, was not familiar with the modern world and did not know that values had changed on the island. He still believed that a man would sell his soul for a red-feather kilt or a dogskin coat.

John had continued to lie and watch the window, because more interesting things might happen.

Indeed, they did.

A voice called to him from below the window.

'Boy! Are you there?'

John sat up and leaned out of the window, looking down.

The bungalow was on stilts which kept it about a metre off the ground. The top of the head of the creature who stood outside was just a little below the sill. John had no name for it. The creature had the body of a man and the head of a dog. It stared at him unblinkingly, while John grappled with his thoughts.

'Boy,' said the dog-headed man. 'Why don't you come for a walk with me?'

John stared at the open mouth of the hound-head and the red tongue lolling sideways. The dog-face was trying to look endearing, as full-bodied dogs often do, but it was hardly working. He looked to John like a sly, crafty cur.

'Why should I?'

'No reason,' said dog-head, 'except we might find some exciting things to do. Have you ever been in an outrigger canoe? We might sail to one of the other islands. Aitutaki for instance.'

Now this *did* interest him. John loved boats and the ocean. It seemed like a scary journey though. The waves were high beyond the reef. It was only the coral which stopped them crashing over the island and washing everything and everyone away.

'Looks a bit stormy out there,' John said, dubiously.

The dog-head turned to stare, then, all of a sudden the sea was calm. Starlight twinkled on the surface. There were dancing wavelets of white foam along the reef, but no giant rollers crashing over the coral.

'How did you do that?' asked John, marvelling.

'Me? I didn't do it. The weather changed, that's all. It does that in the middle of the night. Are you coming now?'

'I don't know. I'll get into awful trouble with Mum. She doesn't like me leaving the house at this hour. She'll get very upset when I'm not in my bed in the morning.'

'Oh,' said dog-face, lightheartedly, 'we'll be back before then.'

This didn't make a great deal of sense.

'But Aitutaki is over 200 kilometres away!'

Dog-head looked a little cross, but then his eyes changed to a soft glow again.

'My canoe is very quick. It skips over the surface of the sea as if propelled by magic.'

'Is it magic?'

'It might be,' replied dog-head, warily. 'Would that bother you?'

'Not at all. I like magic in books, so why shouldn't I like it in real life? You think we can be back before morning? If Mum calls me for breakfast and I'm not here, she'll go berserk.'

'Oh, easily before morning. We'll race the sun back. My canoe can keep ahead of the dawn. You'll see the line of light across the sea, moving rapidly behind us, but it'll never catch or overtake. We can outsail the daybreak and be back here before breakfast. The porpoise will leap over our bows. The dolphins will play in our wake.'

John looked towards the inviting sea. Dog-face's offer was very tempting.

John got out of bed and tiptoed to his mother's room. Her form lay gently breathing under the sheet on her bed. He knew his mother slept very soundly, since she worked hard during the day. She would not wake until the day began to heat up a little.

Back he went then to dog-head, who waited patiently for his return.

'All right,' John said, 'I'm coming.'

He climbed over the windowsill and dropped down next to the strange creature.

'Come on, then,' said dog-face. 'This way.'

John followed, now curious about the creature who had come to lead him on an adventure.

'Who are you?' asked John. '*What* are you?'

'My name is Iskan,' said dog-head, who walked upright, true to his human body. 'I'm one of the older beings of the island. I'm what men call a *Kopuwai*. You won't have heard of our race. We live in the caves in the interior. I only come out – when I want to sail. It's fun sailing on the open sea. I love it.'

John suddenly stopped and looked around him. They were walking on a path into the thick of the rainforest. There were snuffling sounds as they passed the last human dwelling, a pig farm which smelled. It had been the odour which had brought John to his senses. Until then he had been mesmerised by dog-head's voice, by his eyes.

'Where are we going?' asked John. 'We're not heading for the beach at all. We're going into the jungle.'

'Supplies,' said dog-head, quickly. 'We need to stock up with provisions on the boat. What if we get caught out in a storm, or something? We'd have nothing to eat or drink. I keep my supplies up there, on that ridge. We'll get them and bring them down.'

'But I *can't* get caught in a storm. My mother would have a fit if I'm not back in my bed by morning.'

Dog-face laughed, softly. 'Oh, there's not much chance of it at all. We'll be back all right. But you've got to plan for the worst, haven't you? Look at when you got lost in the rainforest, with the Tapairu fairies. You didn't intend to lose your way. It just happened.'

'How did you know about that? And *were* they fairies? I didn't know that.'

'Yes,' growled dog-head, his voice growing more savage by the minute. 'Fairies. Foul fairies, I call them.'

'I thought they were great!'

'You would,' snarled dog-head. 'You're one of – look,' dog-head tried to change the tone of his voice, but hardly succeeded, 'we're nearly at Needle Rock. Just a little climb now. The supplies are stacked at the bottom of the rock. It won't take long.'

John now had grave misgivings. 'I think I'm going back,' he said.

Dog-head's mouth opened in a red-throated roar. His wicked fangs showed row on row back into his mouth. His eyes flashed with hatred and malice.

'NO!' he barked. 'No, no, no. You will please come with me to the rock, my dear young friend. I'll bite the head from your shoulders. I'll rip your arms from their sockets. Nice boy. Come on. I'll give you sweetmeats. I'll tear your legs to shreds, baring them clean to the bone. I'll make you presents of fine weapons of ironwood and turtleshell. A spear. A club. Your mother is there, waiting for you. Your father wants to see you again. He's there too. I'll rip your throat open. Would you like some of the ocean's bounty? Some beautiful cowrie shells. Would you like me to snap off your fingers? I have a sweet bright bird in a cage which would love to go home with you . . .'

The Kopuwai was desperate, letting out a stream of confused words. One moment he was trying to placate John, tempt him with gifts, the next he was threatening him in the most savage way. His voice changed by the second, one sentence coming out with hot foul breath, the next on the back of a mewling, whining tone.

John stepped back, fearful but not panicking. The Kopuwai, formed from the shadow of the kabu, wanted to be nice to the boy. He wanted to persuade him to go further with winning wiles and slippery tongue, but he could not. He was too close to his own grave. His true nature kept rising to the surface, bubbling over. It was impossible not to be his real barbarous self, a creature whose whole being was fashioned from evil, whose hatred of creatures like John was now losing the battle with his desire to get John to the edge of the cliff over the grave.

'No,' said John, turning. 'I'm going home.'

He marched away from the creature with determined step, his face to the onshore breeze, his feet in the direction of the sea.

Then he was suddenly awake, shivering in the night mountain air.

'Where am I?' he whispered to himself. 'I was in bed.'

Gradually it occurred to John that he had been dreaming, and in dreaming he had been sleepwalking. He looked around him at the dark trees and dark crags. What was he doing up here? The palms and other trees flapped in the cool morning air. The dog-headed man from the dream – the Kopuwai – had led him up here. Now it was gone, because it had not been real, it had existed only in John's dream.

John hurried down the mountain path in his pyjamas. He was shaking. The dream had seemed so real, yet he knew he would never have listened to such a weird creature had he been awake. It was only in one's dreams that one took notice of monsters like that. Ordinarily John would have hidden under the sheets and called for his mother.

'I must get back before she wakes,' he muttered to himself, looking behind him every so often to make sure that nothing horrible was following him out of the rainforest. 'I mustn't let her worry.'

John was aware that this job on the island was important to his mother. Her reputation as an archaeologist was growing all the time, but she was not yet fully established. It was not easy for a female Maori to be taken seriously in intellectual circles. Things were changing all the time, for the better, but a female Maori needed to prove her worth. This job on Rarotonga was another stepping-stone towards that proof.

The bungalow came into view. John reached it and climbed back in through the window. He found his bed in the dim room and slipped between the sheets.

There he lay, as the dawn began creeping over the island, like a grey crab across a dark beach. What was happening to him? What did all these incidents mean? He was in great danger, he realised that now, but was it all real or was it because he was actually going mad?

7

Monsters of Sticks and Grass

Being a shadow, the kabu could not do anything physically. Not by himself. But he did have the power of dreams, of hypnotism and of magic. Once a man had been walking back from his village to his home and he met a chicken. The chicken held him with a steady gaze and then led the man, mesmerised, out into the forest and over the edge of a cliff. This had been back in the days when the kabu had not been the half-mad, confused spirit he was today. The man who had died falling from the edge of the cliff had been the descendant of one of those council members who had helped put the sorcerer in his shallow grave.

The sorcerer's kabu was becoming extremely frustrated with the boy, who seemed to slip out of his grasp just when it seemed the kabu had him. The boy's mother was now digging in a place above the sorcerer's tomb. If she discovered his head – the only part of him occupying the grave, since the rest of him had been burnt on a ritual pyre – the sorcerer might be in great trouble. They could do things with his head which would seal his fate forever. His kabu might be a decaying, lost shred of shadowland, but at least it was still out there, seeking.

The kabu now decided that it would create, by magic, a monster of sticks and grass. This *thing* was called a *puatu*. It took the shape of a giant boar which stood on its hind legs. The kabu ordered an evil wind to gather driftwood from the beach; fallen branches from the forest floor for hind legs; thick grasses from the mango swamps to stuff in the hollow parts; mud and stones; a rotten hollow log for a body; dead rats to bulk out the shoulders; spiral shells to make the teeth; pebbles for the eyes.

The wind swirled in the darkness, a crashing whirlwind which ripped branches from the trees and lifted rocks from the ground. It threw these separate parts together, to make the great boar. This terrifying creature stood two metres high on its hind legs and it was horrible in its aspect. Any man with a weak heart who met such an awesome creature, painted with white mud about its jaws and eyes, would no doubt have a cardiac arrest on the spot. It lumbered clumsily through the undergrowth, not seeing but sensing where its victim stood, and it was capable of taking a young boy in its teeth and running off with it. The puatu was going to do just that: deliver John to its master, so that the death blow could be administered with the feathered spear.

This morning happened to be Sunday. There was a church picnic, taking place near Vaka Village. John was going along with Mati and Sally, who had been to one of these events before.

'It's not as boring as you think,' said Sally, as they carried the coolbox full of drinks and chicken sandwiches to the coach. 'There'll be a rock band there – the Surf-Ryders – and knowing how you can dance . . .'

'I didn't think it *would* be boring,' John said, defending himself. 'And I'm not much good at dancing, really.'

'Oh, yes you are,' chimed in Mati. 'Don't forget we've seen you leaping up and down like a madman.'

John shook his head. 'There's different kinds of dancing. I can only do one kind, and I didn't even know I could do *that* until the other night.'

Sally said, 'You're too modest. If you can do one kind of dance, you can do another.'

John saw that it was useless to argue with his friends, so he said nothing further. He had other problems at the moment. There was a boy called Ika who fancied Sally and thought of her as his girlfriend. Ika must have felt he could handle Mati trailing around after Sally, but a newcomer was something else. John had only been on the island five minutes and here he was monopolising Sally's time. Ika saw this as an affront. He was a broadshouldered lad, muscled from rowing canoes and swimming, and he stood slightly taller than John. On one or two occasions recently Ika had tried to get John into a fight with him.

Ika was also on the picnic. As John boarded the coach behind Sally, Ika tried to trip him up. The coolbox clattered in the aisle as John stumbled, causing the coach driver to turn.

'Watch what you do with them snegs, boy,' said the driver.

Snegs? What were snegs?

'I don't know what you mean,' John said, kicking at Ika's outstretched ankle. 'What snegs?'

Ika avoided the kick with a grin on his face, happy to see John caught up in something he did not understand.

Mati came to his rescue. 'He means the sandwiches and drink, in the cool box. Snacks.'

'Well, why doesn't he say so?'

The driver glared. 'I did. Don't you understand English?'

Some of the other children on the bus laughed. Ika

laughed louder than any of them. 'Idiot!' he cried at John. *'No 'ea mai koe?'*

If he thought he was going to intimidate John with the local language Ika was mistaken. John had learned a lot.

'I'm from New Zealand, where nobody uses daft words like "sneg" – all right?'

'It's just the accent,' whispered Sally. 'That's how some of the islanders say it here. Don't make a big thing, John.'

John decided Sally was right. He found a seat and sat down heavily. His blood was boiling. Ika was spoiling for a battle. Well, John was mad enough to give him one. Nobody called him an idiot and laughed at him without paying for it. John was going to wait his chance on the picnic, then offer to fight Ika somewhere out of sight of the adults. John couldn't take these insults any more without retaliating.

When the Surf-Ryders were well into their third number, John went up to Ika and glared into his face. They both knew what it meant. Ika detached himself from a group, though he was followed by one or two of his closest friends. John walked off into the undergrowth, having found a patch which suited his purpose. Mati came with him.

Sally was dancing with another girl in front of the band, having no idea what was going on. John didn't want her there. He wasn't sure he was going to win and anyway Sally wouldn't have approved of what was going on even if he did, so it was best to keep it amongst the boys.

'So?' said Ika, confronting him with hands on hips, 'what do *you* want, new kid?'

'He's not new any more,' chipped in Mati.

'You keep out of this, unless you want to lose some teeth too. I'm talkin' to the new kid, here, who doesn't understand nothin'. Well, new kid? Deaf and dumb, or what?'

John answered by punching Ika in the chest and sending him sprawling on his backside in the dust. The blow hurt John's knuckles, bringing water to his eyes. But he was fiery mad now. He wanted to make Ika bawl. He wanted that more than anything in the world.

Ika looked surprised, but jumped to his feet immediately.

'Right,' he said. 'You've done it now.'

He leapt on John and delivered several blows to his face. John's nose felt like it was exploding. He lashed out himself, catching the other boy on the side of the head, behind his ear, twice. Ika reeled away, panting and choking in fury. He kicked out at John, but missed, and overbalanced. John waited for him to get to his feet. John's nose was bleeding profusely now, and Ika's ear was swelling visibly before the audience.

One of Ika's friends suddenly crouched behind John, so that Ika could push him over, but Mati stepped in and dusted the boy's pants with his sandalled foot, sending him on to his face in the dirt.

'None of that,' said Mati. 'One on one. Once were warriors, not cheats and cowards.'

Ika tried a swing at John, while John's attention was on this exchange behind his back. John ducked and the fist swished over his right shoulder. He punched out again, his hard little fist striking Ika on the same spot on his chest as before. He must have bruised his opponent the first time, because Ika showed pain in his expression. He stepped back and rubbed himself through his T-shirt.

'Is that all you can do?' snapped Ika. 'Hit people in the biggest part of their body?'

'Seems like good sense to me,' muttered Mati.

All the fire had gone out of the two fighters now. They seemed pretty evenly matched and any blow from one would be countered with a strike from the other. There wasn't a lot of point in beating each other into the dust, both getting hurt, and no winner arising. So they stood there and traded insults for a short while. It was during this tirade that a noise was heard in the bushes nearby. Mati called for silence.

'Listen!' he said. 'There's someone in there.'

John was suspicious. 'Is that you, Sally?' he called.

He snuffled on the blood from his nose, which was beginning to dry up.

There was no proper answer. Just more rustling and the clacking of stone on stone.

Ika said, 'Sounds like something – a wild pig.'

The boys were always talking about the possible existence of wild pigs in the rainforest. They had visions of themselves hunting these mythical creatures and taking home the bacon to their proud parents. They told each other – though none had actually *seen* the animals – that there were many such pigs to be found – offspring of long-ago escaped livestock. Even amongst the adults such stories abounded, just as they talked about huge fish that remained uncaught in mountain ponds and magnificent game birds that were waiting to be trapped or shot.

Ika picked up a heavy rock. Mati did the same. Soon most of the boys were armed with stones.

'Wait!' said John. 'It might be someone. You can't just throw bricks at bushes without finding out what's in there.'

Ika said, 'All right, *you* go and look first. But don't blame us if you get gored or bitten.'

John was naturally reluctant to do this.

'I didn't say it *wasn't* a pig,' he argued. 'I just said it might not be.'

'I'll come with you,' said Mati. 'We'll go behind it and chase it out – I'm not scared.'

He clearly was, being pale with fright, but John nodded.

'Horns of the buffalo,' he said. They had seen the film *Zulu Dawn* the week before, where the Zulus defeated the British Army with their classic buffalo shape attack. 'You go round one way, and I'll go the other.'

John picked up a stout stick from the ground and crept to the right of the bushes in question, circling round. Mati went to the left. The other boys, some twelve or so, waited in the clearing. Apart from a few lingering pains on the combatants the fight was largely forgotten. Important now was the hunt. They were about to kill a wild pig. No one could remember when that was last done. Hunting wild pigs had gone out with making fire from spinning a hardwood stick on a softwood base filled with copra. Now everyone bought matches and pork chops from the supermarket. They would be heroes, even amongst some of the adults. This was the old way, the way of their ancestors. They could roast the pig over a charcoal fire on the beach and feast on its fat!

John and Mati closed in on the set of bushes where the sound was coming from.

Suddenly, out of the thicket came the wild pig, a huge beast on its hind legs. It made a loud grating sound in its throat, like two rocks rubbing together.

Mati screamed. He dropped his 'weapon' and ran back to the other boys. John was left to face the giant puatu alone.

8
A Shattering Experience

The giant makeshift boar had two great curving tusks coming from its clay mouth. They were made of broken branches and they swept outwards and upwards, bark-stripped-white with stubs and knots, jagged at their broken ends. Lumbering forward the beast of sticks-and-stones tried to gather up John with these tusks. Though terrified, John managed to dart behind a tree. He moved round, away from the advance of the creature, keeping the trunk between himself and its gaping maw.

'Keep away from me!' yelled John. 'Go away!'

Despite being a thing of mud and straw, the boar was solidly fashioned. He crashed into the trunk of the tree and made it shudder to its very roots. The tusks came one either side of the trunk, missing John's head by centimetres. Twice more the frustrated beast withdrew and then smashed its bulk into the trunk, its clay snout snorting with rage. John no longer felt safe where he was. The tree behind which he stood was weakening. He dashed for the path through the bushes.

The beast was after him in an instant. It ran awkwardly, its bough legs thumping on the hard earth, its sharply-ridged chest heaving with the effort. Bits of earth and turf fell from it as it ran, scattering fragments of itself over the landscape. But the speed with which it moved was incredible. John knew he could not outrun it. John shinned up a stronger-looking tree with low branches, climbing like a monkey for his life.

Once more the beast growled in that rock-grating way and charged the tree trunk. John was shaken from the branches and fell to the ground at the creature's feet. It scooped him up in its tusks, gripped him with a mouth of wood and stone, and prepared to make off with him.

'Help!' cried John.

At that moment Mati returned with the other kids. The children stood at the edge of the clearing, peering through the shafts of sunlight at the horrible creature who held John in its mouth.

John continued to struggle, more through fear than anything else.

Ika suddenly cried out, 'What the hell is that?'

'A monster,' said Mati, a little unnecessarily.

Ika seemed the calmest of the lot. He picked up a rock from the ground. 'Go for its legs,' he told the others. He threw the stone and struck the beast on one of its bough hind limbs.

Automatically – for Ika was one of those natural leaders amongst his peers – the other kids picked up stones and began to throw them, aiming for the beast's legs. Heavy rocks began to strike its limbs. It tottered this way and that, the stones raining on it so thickly it wasn't able to build up its run from the glade. Then a very heavy stone hit it about where an ankle would be, if it had owned ankles. The bough leg was knocked askew, dislocated at the joint. The beast growled loudly, stepped sideways, and crashed heavily to the ground. John rolled free from its jaws. The boy scrambled to his feet and joined his rescuers.

A great cheer went up from the kids who, scared as they were, realised they now had the advantage.

The shower of stones continued to fall on the boar. Bits flew off it as it was struck: a branch here, a lump of clay there. Its turf shoulders crumbled under the onslaught. It seemed that once a single part of it had been dislodged, other parts loosened, like taking that first brick from a wall and weakening it so that others could be prised out. An upper limb cracked and split. One of the tusks was struck and flew out, spinning like a boomerang, landing on the forest floor yards away.

The beast let out a moaning cry of despair: the sort of sound that a dying buffalo might make. The children were merciless. They picked up heavy dead branches from the ground and went in for the kill, John amongst them. They surrounded the boar and whacked it with their clubs, breaking it up completely, scattering its various bits over the glade. When they finally stopped, they were all panting with the exertion. John was running with perspiration. They all stood there, breathing heavily, staring at the place where the creature had been.

Ika said in an unsteady voice, 'That'll teach it.'

'Yes,' muttered Sally, 'but what *was* it? And why did it attack Mati and John?'

'It was a wild beast,' Mati said. 'It'd attack anyone.'

Sally, not from the island, wasn't going to accept this.

'It *wasn't* a wild beast. It was something made up of bits of nature. Just branches and tufts of grass and chunks of rock. I mean, I was really scared. You think it was some kind of robot, but made up of sticks and stones, instead of metal? Someone must have made it, mustn't they? It's got to be a machine or something, hasn't it? Maybe with a remote control, like Mati's model car . . .'

She stared around, looking up into the trees, as if expecting to sight some joker fiddling with an electronic device.

John wasn't sure. 'But where's its motor? If it's robotic, it's got to have some sort of engine, hasn't it?'

Ika kicked at the remains of sticks and stones at his feet.

'There's nothing like that here. Just bits of wood.'

Sally was not to be thwarted. 'Maybe we smashed it to bits? Maybe it was some sort of computerised device – you know how small they make those things these days. Maybe we whacked it with a rock and broke it? Let's look for it.'

She and some of the other kids began sorting through the debris on the forest floor. Mati, Ika and John did not join them. These three seemed to know there was no remote controller, no programmed computer device driving the monster. In their hearts the boys knew this was a supernatural creature.

'I'm going to get my dad,' said Mati. 'You lot wait here.'

He went off and fetched a group of parents. The kids told them they had been attacked by a *thing* made of sticks and stones, turf and clay, bits of fern and grass. The adults raised their eyebrows. They asked to be shown the remains of the creature. When bits of twig and mud were produced they frowned.

'Is this some sort of joke?' asked Mati's dad.

Sally misunderstood. 'That's just what I said,' she cried. 'I think someone's having a joke with us. Someone's hiding in the trees somewhere. Should we go and look?'

'I mean, are you fooling with us?' Mati's dad suddenly grinned. 'You're making all this up, aren't you? What, is this get-back-at-parents week, or what? We're not daft you know.'

One of the mothers said, 'Look, the ants will be getting at the picnic. I'm sure all this is very funny, but the food's out and ready to be eaten.'

The adults began muttering amongst themselves and drifted out of the glade, back towards the picnic site. Mati's dad remained, kicking through the debris. 'You kids,' he said.

Mati was defiant. 'Really Dad. It was like some kind of nightmare. It was a monster. We all saw it. All of us kids.'

There was nodding from the children and one of them looked as if he was about to burst into tears.

'It grabbed John you say?' murmured Mati's dad. 'You didn't just mistake the shadows – the sunlight coming through the trees? In these forests it's easy to see things that aren't really there, you know.'

Ika said, 'John was off the ground. You can't get away from that. He was lifted up. Shadows don't lift people.'

'But you might have *thought* . . .'

John cried, 'It had me. It was real. I ought to know.'

Clearly the children had witnessed something very

strange. Mati's dad didn't know what it was, but assured them he would inform the island police.

'Let them come out here and look around. Maybe they'll find some sort of explanation for it,' he told the children. 'I don't know. I'll have a word with them. They might think I'm crazy, but these things ought to be reported.'

When John got home that evening he was still trembling. His mother noticed his paleness and shaking. 'Are you not well?' she said.

'I'm scared,' he muttered. He told her what had happened.

Mary Terangi was a sympathetic mother. Her first thought was that her son was traumatised and going through some sort of mental problem, probably associated with moving house and home. She listened to the whole story, offered a number of plausible explanations, none of which she saw accepted by her son. Then she gently pointed out that such a thing was not possible: a beast of sticks and stones coming to life.

'Ask the other kids,' John said, gloomily.

She did just that, calling on them in their homes. They all had the same story. It was incredible, but they had definitely had some sort of experience which had left them all terrified. Ika had also appeared elated. He and his army had defeated the monster. They had broken it to bits and saved John's life. He felt they should be treated like heroes.

Mary assured him he was a hero for not running away in such a situation.

'Thank you for saving John,' she said. 'I'm not sure from what, but clearly there was some kind of creature there.'

She and Mati's dad visited the police station. Policemen and policewomen, in general, are very solid sensible characters. They do not need wild and wonderful imaginations to be accepted into the police force: in fact the sort of talents which make fortunes for writers and artists are discouraged by the police authorities. They are expected to be stolid, hard-working females or fellows, with little or no belief in the supernatural, otherwise burglars and others of the criminal profession would be pleading innocent all the time, saying they were forced to steal by the fairies, or the giants, or the monsters of the forest.

The police listened, wrote things in a ledger, and said they would go out and look at the spot, and perhaps interview the children.

They really had no intention of looking anywhere.

'How can we take this further?' asked Mary of Mati's dad. 'We can't just let it drop. The children were clearly scared by something. Isn't there anyone else we can go to?'

'Who?' asked Mati's dad. 'Authorities on the island

are thin on the ground. I'll go out again with my brother and have another look. Otherwise I think we'd better just assure the kids that something unusual happened which won't occur again.'

'Can we be sure of that? That it won't happen again?'

Clearly at a loss, Mati's dad shrugged his shoulders. 'Since I don't really know what happened, I don't know. But we can't have the kids walking around like zombies, scared of their own shadows. Let's just hope this is an isolated incident and try to forget it.'

John, of course, could not forget it. He was beginning to think the island was haunted in some way, and that the spirits who were doing the haunting were out to get him especially. The other kids were viewing him in much the same light. Although Mati was sure that if the monster hadn't gone for John, it would have attacked *him* instead, he was willing to admit that none of this stuff happened before John came to the island.

'One thing's certain,' he told John, 'it's not my gran'mam that's doing all this.'

John rolled his eyes. 'I kind of worked that out for myself, thanks, Mati.'

'Well, you never know with these dead people,' Mati said, sagely. 'They can be very tricky.'

Out in the forest, the kabu fumed. Its plans for grasping this fairy boy and sacrificing him were not going as smoothly as it wished. Madness was in the soul-shadow's mind. Its thoughts were caught in a dark sea of eddies and currents, whirling, swirling, forming crested waves and crashing down on the empty grey beaches of lost islands. There was no colour in its thinking: all was bleak grey, black and white. Somewhere deep within it a wailing sound was building in volume, which would come screaming out of the hole where its mouth should be. At that moment all hope would be gone, all desires dead. The sorcerer's body, its home, would never rise again from its earthen grave, to walk the island paths, to strike fear into its people, to start again its reign of terror.

9
A Temple and a Storm

'What are you actually looking for?' asked John, standing with his mother at her dig beside Needle Rock.

'It's said there's the grave of a sorcerer somewhere around the rock. A man named Makke-te, who ruled the island during a dark period of its history.'

'I thought kings ruled the island.'

'Well, they did, but this man Makke-te invoked powerful sorcery. It's said he poisoned the king at the time. Being ruthless and greatly feared for his dark magic, he was able to move into a position of absolute rulership. The stories passed down by word of mouth say that Makke-te's ceremonial hut was made out of human bones and decorated with the skulls of those he had tortured and put to death.'

John was fascinated by this character out of Rarotonga's past.

'Why do you want to dig him up?'

'Actually, we believe his body was burned. Only his head is supposed to be in the tomb, along with his weapons. A ritual arrow or short spear and a horrible dagger called an *airo fai.*'

John stared down into the square pits that were appearing around Needle Rock. His mother, dressed in slacks and shirt, was busy with a trowel and a powder brush, even as she talked. There were two men with her, marking out a new area with spikes and string.

John asked, 'What was so bad about this dagger thing?'

'The airo fai? It was such a horrible weapon only priest-shamans were permitted to use them, for ritual killings. They were made out of a stingray's backbone. There are tiny bones, like fishing hooks, which run down a stingray's spine. When the airo fai is thrust into a victim's stomach, these hooks catch on to the flesh inside, so that when it's wrenched out again, it rips out the victim's innards. Pretty gory, eh?'

Mary did not believe in mincing words with her son, when she was explaining aspects of her work. Had he been a few years younger, she might have curbed her description, but she felt he was old enough to know the truth about the nasty side of life. Juveniles, Mary had decided, tended to view violence with detached interest. Such things happened in the distant past, but could not happen today. They belonged to another place and time and were not threatening in any way.

'Cool!' said John, probably because it was expected of him. 'Have you ever found one before?'

'An airo fai? No. I've seen a drawing of one, made by a nineteenth-century British sailor, but I've not handled one. That's why I want to find it so badly. It will go into the Auckland Museum, initially, because there it'll be seen by more people. But it'll only be there on loan. From time to time it'll come back here to the smaller Rarotongan Museum, which will actually own it.'

'Be a big coup for you, eh, Mum?'

His mother looked up at him, fondly. 'Yes, it would.'

She did not know it, but John was hoping she would find the grave of the sorcerer's head very soon. Much as he loved the beauty and friendliness of the island, he was aware he was being subjected to its supernatural elements. John didn't want to tell his mother he felt haunted. It would worry her and she would probably abandon her work and take him back to New Zealand. John didn't doubt that she would fuss over him there and perhaps make him go to a doctor. Like most adults Mary always looked for rational scientific explanations to phenomena, while John was able to sense, yes even smell, the evil pursuing him.

'I think I'll go home, Mum. I hope you find it soon.'

'All right, dear. And thanks for the encouragement.'

John started off along the path, down towards the small town. He had walked this track many times now and knew it quite well. Part of the journey was through a tunnel of leafy trees which overhung the path and obscured it from the sunlight. It was naturally dark in this tunnel at all times of the day, but when John felt he was emerging from the other end, there was no bright opening of light. It still remained very dim.

In fact, while he had been inside the tunnel, the weather seemed to have changed. Huge black storm clouds had rolled over the island. The wind had picked up and was now whipping the trees back and forth with a violence John had not witnessed previously. Clearly a storm was coming in from the ocean, bringing salt spray with it, even into the hinterland. The salt stung his eyes as he walked, head down, trying to keep sight of the track and not lose his way in the murk.

Once the sun was blocked out, Rarotonga was a different world. It appeared smaller and less tame. Soon the lack of light was so bad John could not see the ocean ahead of him. Fronds lashed at his face as he fought his way along the narrow path. It had also grown very cold and dressed in shorts and a thin shirt, he was soon wet and shivering.

Eventually John stumbled over some stones, which he realised were part of a crumbled building. Crouching down behind the moss-covered wall, he attempted to keep his body out of the path of the wind. As he stared around him in the gloom, he noticed dour faces staring back at him. They had holes for eyes, and mouths open as if about to howl, and some had large ears, pinned back against their long narrow skulls.

Were they looking at him?

After the first shock he realised the gnarled and pitted heads were actually made of wood and stone – ancient carvings – and they were probably on sacred ground, planted at all angles, some having fallen on their backs or sides. He was in the ruins of some old temple, covered in vines, creepers and moss, and the faces belonged to ancient gods, ancestors of the Polynesians, and demi-god-heroes.

John shuddered under their openmouthed gaze. They were not the most pleasant-looking characters. Some had actually been carved with the intention of striking fear and horror into the hearts of believers. Where the wood had been eaten away by insects, the ugliness of each individual visage was now exaggerated. On the stone carvings, moss and fungi had grown, forming swollen ears and noses, mutating the original work.

'You're an ugly bunch of characters,' muttered John, trying to keep his spirits up. But his words sounded very hollow amongst the tumbled walls and scattered stones. His own voice had the ability to frighten him.

The wind was increasing in strength, screaming

through the crags above the forest, wailing in the treetops. John hunched himself in a small hollow, hoping there was nothing in the damp grasses which would bite him. He couldn't remember if there were scorpions on Rarotonga or not. He didn't think so, but he was unsure enough to be concerned.

Suddenly, he was aware that one of the faces in front of him was not of stone or wood. A man sat opposite him, naked apart from a loin cloth. Half of his body was covered in tattoos: the kind of markings John had seen on old pictures of Maori chiefs: the other half was in shadow but appeared to be clear of tattoos. The shape of the face was lean and there were two penetrating eyes that bore into John's own.

'Aaahhh!' cried John, stiffening his back against the wall behind him. 'What – what are you doing?'

'Don't be afraid,' said the man. 'This was a wise place to seek sanctuary from the storm. A secret temple. There are many of these, you know, hidden in the rainforest. Most of them have disappeared altogether, under the ravages of time and nature.'

John was aware that the man was talking in Polynesian, his long yellow teeth clacking as he spoke. John's command of the language was not yet brilliant, but he had seen studying hard lately and was able to follow the gist of what was being said to him. He replied in the same tongue.

'I'm – I'm not afraid. You startled me.'

'I wish to lead you back – to your mother,' said the man, rising. 'Will you follow me?'

John saw that his companion had an easy grace about him. His movements were fluid and smooth. Could he trust this man? They were caught in the heart of a storm. It seemed sensible to stay where they were for the time being. If they walked there was a danger of being hit by falling branches, or even trees. Yet the desire to be with his mother, and safety, was overwhelming. John got to his feet.

'Who are you?' he asked. 'What's your name?'

The man glared. 'Don't you know it's offensive to ask someone his name? What if I were someone famous? You would be insulting me by admitting you did not know who I am. I might be a hero. Or I might be a common fisherman, ashamed of my lowly status. You should never ask a stranger his name. You should wait until he offers it.'

'I'm sorry,' mumbled John. 'I didn't know.'

'Are you a Maori, or not?'

'I have Maori ancestors, yes.'

'Then you should know these things.'

John now did remember having been told something of the sort, when he had studied Maori history in New Zealand. But it was difficult to remember everything. History, to a young boy, is dry dusty stuff, especially when it involves outmoded manners and etiquette.

John found himself following the man through a rainforest whipped by slim winds. The darkness was still very dense, even though somewhere above the clouds the sun was still shining. A misty mizzle was now lashing into the trees. It seemed the world had gone mad. Not knowing where he was going John trod in the direction of the man going before him, wondering at the lightness of his step, for he seemed to leave no depression on the masty forest floor, while John sank into it, leaving deep footprints wherever he trod.

'How do you do that?' he asked at length. 'Is it some kind of trick?'

'Do what?' asked the man.

'How do you manage to skip over the top of the dead leaves?'

'I am a fire-walker. We have a very light tread. Otherwise we would burn our feet.'

That made sense, but did not completely satisfy John. After all, this was defying gravity, wasn't it? But then the man looked very skinny and perhaps weighed very little. He was certainly no taller than John. If he had the knack of floating while he walked, well John should be curious but impressed, rather than suspicious.

'I wish I could do that,' he said to the man.

Unexpectedly, John's companion turned and grinned, distorting his tattoos.

'Perhaps very soon you will be able to.'

Then he turned and continued along the narrow path.

John wondered what he meant by those words. Was he going to be taught the trick of fire-walking? But he was soon worrying about something else. His fear of injury or death from falling branches and trees was very real. In a dense forest such dangers are not rare. During a high wind or storm they are obviously even more frequent. A tree crashed down only yards away from the path, fortunately getting caught up in other trees on its way down and remaining at an angle above the ground.

'Hey!' said John. 'That was close.'

'You need have no fear,' muttered the man. 'I won't let any harm come to you . . .'

The sentence seemed unfinished and John wondered what further words might be added to this cold comfort. And after all, how could this thin brittle-looking man stop a tree from falling on them? That didn't make sense. It was all very silly. John stopped walking.

'I'm going back,' he said. 'I don't know why we left that old temple. It was safer than being in the open.'

The man whirled, angrily.

'You will follow me!' he ordered. 'I'm responsible for you. If something happens to you they will blame me. I demand you keep to the path.'

John blinked and stepped back from the fury.

'I – I think – I can decide for myself. I don't know you.'

The man stared through the gloom, then his manner changed completely, in an instant.

'You should listen to your elders,' he replied, gently, revealing the long peg-shaped teeth again. His head looked very skull-like in the dimness, with only a few wispy hairs hanging from his scalp. 'I know the way. It's quite safe.'

'It can't be safe with trees and branches falling all the time.'

'We're nearly there,' pleaded the man. 'Not far now.'

'Not far from where?'

'From the Needle. Your mother is there. The rock will protect you.'

John saw some sense in this. 'All right. But we ought to get a move on.'

The figure in front hardly seemed to turn at all. He suddenly appeared to face the other way without moving. Then he was walking again, calling back to John to follow quickly, and that their journey's end was near.

10

Play me a Tune, and Die

The head of Makke-te sensed the presence of the fairy-boy. The tapairu child was standing above the grave, talking with Makke-te's kabu, now in the form of a shadowman.

At last! At last he had one of his hated enemies within his thrall! This child was not of pure fairy blood, but long ago in the past one of the child's ancestors had lain with a fairy. Whole fairy, part fairy, it didn't matter. The magic called for the ritual killing of a sorcerer's greatest enemy. The boy had the blood of that enemy in his veins.

Once the killing had taken place, the head would grow another body and Makke-te could walk the island once again, sowing terror in the night, gathering power to himself. Once again mankind would fear his name, would wake sweating in their beds, would die with their eyes starting from their heads and their mouths locked open in one last horrible scream.

Makke-te recalled those past times when his voice spoke like a drum and men turned to statues in his presence, for fear of offending him. In those days he had been king of the breadfruit, the lord of taro, yam and sweet potato, the prince of sacrificed pigs. He had owned huts and temples by the dozen, built for him by his slaves. There were those whose job it was to waft away the flies from his person. There were those who cooked his food and those who put it in his mouth. There were great canoes built in his honour, and statues carved, and sacrificial platforms raised, and great banquets of meat: the flesh of killed enemies.

Oh, to taste the flesh of man again! He had savoured it in his dreams. Now those dreams were to become real.

Dig, boy, dig, said Makke-te. *Find the implement of your death, planted by a loyal slave in my own time.*

Soon, the dagger which lay in the grave beside Makke-te, the airo fai, would be plunging into abdomens and tearing out the innards of disobedient servants, disloyal men and women.

And Makke-te would form an army to hunt down the hated Tapairu, the fairies of the forest, and so rid himself of the creatures who had been his downfall the first time.

But first the boy had to find the bamboo flute, within which was the small ritual spear, a dart, fletched with red feathers. When the end of the flute was pressed against or by something – a mouth, a hand, an eye – a spring would release the weapon inside. It would fly forth and pierce the victim, injecting him or her with a deadly poison.

Such was the method by which death was delivered.

John could hear the voice of his mother, high above him on the ridge which bore the needle of rock on its crest.

'There she is,' he said. 'How do I get up to her?'

The tattooed kabu was growing impatient.

'Never mind her. Look what you're standing on.'

John looked down at where the tattooed man was pointing and saw a huge green stone, roughly carved in the shape of a shark. It was dirty and greasy, from the natural oils of the marshy ground, but John could see that the carving had a mouth half-buried in the earth. The whole thing was much too large and heavy to lift, but the kabu urged John to dig away the soil which filled the mouth of the shark.

'My mother would like this carving,' said John.

'No, no, this is not a man-made thing, it has been fashioned by the elements, by nature. The wind and rain have attacked this stone and the shape of the shark is an accident, just as clouds seem to resemble beasts and birds, so too rock and stones, especially on volcanic islands such as this. Your mother is only interested in artefacts.'

John nodded. 'That's true. But why should I dig in the mouth of this thing? I don't like the look of it.'

'You might find something to your advantage.'

'What?'

But the man was drifting away now. He seemed to fade into the trees behind him and John was left standing there, wondering. His first instinct was to shout up to his mother, but something stopped him. A few moments later he found himself digging in the mouth of the shark, shovelling the moist earth away with his hands. It was not long before he came upon an object and withdrew it from the shark's mouth.

'It's only a bamboo tube,' he said to himself, disappointed. 'So what?'

But when he wiped the half-metre long tube free of dirt he saw that it was covered in strange markings, etchings, and there were holes running along it.

'Wow!' muttered John. 'This is probably just the sort of thing Mum's looking for!'

He shook the bamboo tube and it rattled. Inspecting one end he found it to be blocked. The other end though, was open.

As with any tube bearing unknown contents, the instinct is to hold it up and look into it. John lifted the tube and found it to be surprisingly heavy. He peered into the open end, but of course he could see nothing in the darkness within. He shook it again, as he tried to see what was inside, but though it rattled in reply, he could still see nothing. When he held it up to the sun however, he realised that holes running down it let the light in sufficiently for him to see what was inside.

Perhaps if he pressed his eye to the open end, like a telescope, he might be able to . . .

'John?'

John whirled in surprise, to find Sally and Mati standing behind him, grinning.

'We came up looking for you,' said Mati, 'after the storm, but your mum said you'd gone home. Then Sally saw you from up there.'

He pointed to Needle Rock.

'It's a steep climb down here,' said Sally, looking at her dirty hands. 'You've got to hang on to tree roots and things. I nearly fell twice.'

Mati said, 'Your mum's gone home now. Are you coming back? We're going to look for shells on the beach. There's always a lot after a storm. The waves throw them up on to the sand.'

'Shells?'

'Yes,' said Sally, 'cowries, green turbans, wentletraps, combs, strawberry tops, bishop's mitres, you name it.'

'Conches?' John asked.

Mati shook his head. 'They're too big to be chucked up by waves – but anything smaller. Bits of coral too.'

'I thought that wasn't allowed – conservation and all that?'

'It's all right to take shells and coral from the beach. They're dead then. It's when they're still in the sea they're taboo. What's that you've got there? That hunk of bamboo?'

'Oh, this?' John said. 'I found it. It's got some funny markings on it. I think it's an ancient artefact. I was going to give it to Mum.'

'It's got holes down it,' said Sally. 'I bet it's a musical instrument.'

Mati took the flute. 'Have you tried to blow it?' He lifted it towards his mouth, but saw Sally grimacing.

'What's the matter?' he asked.

'What's the matter? You boys! That thing is *filthy*. It's probably got all sorts of germs. That's what's the matter.'

Mati looked dubiously at the flute, then handed it back to John.

'We'd better wash it first,' he said. 'Then we can have a go.'

'Soak it in a light solution of bleach,' Sally advised, primly. 'That'll kill any germs on it. After all, you don't know who the last person was who blew that thing. He might have had TB. Don't you know the tubercle bacillus can live in the soil for years and years and still infect you? What do you two dream about during biology class?'

'Miss Know-it-all,' muttered Mati.

'Ms Know-it-all, if you don't mind,' corrected Sally. 'And yes I do, because I want to pass my exams. You should be thinking about that too! The trouble with boys is they've got their heads full of sport.'

Mati found John a piece of string in his pocket and John tied the ends to the flute, then slung it across his shoulders. The three friends climbed back up to Needle Rock and made their way to the beach.

Sure enough the storm had tossed weed and shells and cuttlefish bones up on to the shore, to be sorted through by the kids. Most of the children on the island collected seashells, for the islands of the Pacific are rich in the bounty tossed up by the ocean. There were thousands of different kinds of shells, all very beautiful, with intricate patterns and shapes, and since they were freshly dead and had not lain in the sun long, their colours and sheen were still bright. There is nothing like collecting things to obsess a young man. Stamps, matchbox tops, shells, it really doesn't matter what, so long as there is a search, an occasional great find, and a display of collected treasures to show people.

The flute was forgotten in the enthusiastic seeking of shells.

When John got home he threw the flute in his bedroom cupboard and took a box of shells to show his mother.

She ooo-ed and aahhh-ed as a mother should, emphasised that nothing *live* should be taken from the ocean, and the evening passed pleasantly until the going down of the sun.

Makke-te was incensed. Surely the boy should have been curious enough about the sound of the flute to at least try a single note? Any fairy worth its salt would have instantly placed the instrument to its lips and attempted to blow a tune. Perhaps the child's blood had been weakened by the human in him to a point beyond the pale? Yet, Makke-te knew that the youth was his last chance and patience was the watchword. It was difficult to be patient with several centuries of a dark grave above his head, but Makke-te was doing his level best.

Damn the fairies. He could hear them even now. Playing their own fickle tunes.

Indeed, deep in the forest that night, the Tapairu were doing just that. Their flutes, pipes, and other musical instruments were whistling lilting tunes, dancing tunes, which had the fairies of the forest on their feet and tripping through the moonbeams.

Makke-te could hear his old enemies and he hated them for the joy which was in their hearts. Dancing was not about delight! In Makke-te's opinion it should be a prelude to death, a sinister terrifying artform, with mystic steps and meaningful looks. Dances should have victims, not willing participants. The fairies, as usual, were warping the true sense of the culture of the island in not allowing fear to flourish!

An owl with a human face came to rest on the windowsill of John's bedroom, perched there in the shadows of the night.

'Wouldn't you like to play a tune, son?' said the owl in the voice of Mary Terangi. 'Just a gentle rustling kind of song? One such as the wind blows through the leaves of the trees, or one such as the waters of a stream composes while gushing over the stones of its bed?'

'What?' murmured John, half-awake, half-asleep. 'Who's that? Is that you, Mum?'

'Just me, son, come to encourage a little night music.'

John tried to open his eyes, but he had had a long weary day, and the effort was too much.

'In the morning, Mum. I'll play it in the morning.'

In a few moments John was in a deep sleep and the defeated owl clacked its hook beak, spread its wings, and took to the darkness.

11

Visitors in the Night

John woke the next morning and immediately remembered his shells. When he went out on to the veranda, where he had left them in a bucket, he hit a horrible smell as solid as a wall.

Mati came over before breakfast as usual.

'You're supposed to bury them in the garden,' he explained. 'The storm killed the molluscs inside, but you need to get the ants to eat them clean. They're rotting at the moment and there's nothing worse than the stink of rotting sea creatures, I can tell you.'

He didn't need to tell John. The odour penetrated every part of the bungalow. Mary was complaining loudly from the kitchen.

'Get rid of them! I can't eat my breakfast.'

The two boys buried the shells not far from

gran'mam's grave. Even before a light covering of soil was put over them there was a long line of big black ants moving in on the food.

'Buryin' 'em won't hurt 'em,' explained Mati. 'If you tried to boil 'em, you'd spoil the glaze on the shells – and the colour. This way, once they're clean, they'll stay good forever. My mam has got a pair of tiger cowries on her dresser which she found when she was six. They look as good as new. Could've been found yesterday. Course, she took 'em straight from the lagoon, but they didn't know any better in those days. It was all right then, anyway, 'cos they ate the creatures inside, sometimes raw . . .'

Since the smell of the rotting molluscs still lingered, the thought of eating them raw made John's stomach turn over.

After breakfast the two boys went on a cycle ride, to collect Sally. There was a sponsored round-the-island ride that day, being Saturday, to collect money for the local hospital. The ride was in the morning, before the sun got too high. After that the kids all went down to the lagoon for a cooling-off swim, before a late salad lunch at Trader Jacks, paid for by the organisers of the cycle ride.

It was only when evening came that John remembered his find in the forest the day before.

'The flute,' he said. 'I still haven't washed it.'

Sally wrinkled her nose. 'Well don't try to play it

before you've given it a thorough soaking. Personally, I wouldn't want to put that thing to my mouth. Think of all the slugs and snails that've slid over it, while it's been in the ground. Yuk!'

John cycled the last half-mile through Avarua alone. Past Para O Tane Palace, home of the Ariki, or chief of Avarua. Past the Seven-in-One coconut tree, and on towards home. The sun was a big red disc slipping behind Te Manga peak, beyond Maungatea Bluff. John stopped and watched it disappear, which it did very quickly at this latitude. After this he was riding in darkness, swishing past oleander bushes, and under the palms where huge fruit bats roosted for the night.

Suddenly, and shockingly, there was a figure running beside John's bike, as he went up the track towards the bungalow.

It was the tattooed man from the forest.

'When are you going to play your flute?'

John almost fell off his cycle, which wobbled dangerously.

'Where did you come from?' he cried.

'Oh, I've been here and there. I saw you. I thought I'd run beside that – that . . .' here the tattooed man faltered and stopped. John could see he did not know the name of the machine on which John was riding. *He obviously did not know what a bicycle was*. And now that he was outside the forest, the man looked very strange, almost a patchwork of pieces of darkness, a thing of tattered shadows. There was no light in him at all, only different shades. John now saw the evil seeping from this creature's tattooed skin, as one might see gleaming sweat on an animal's hide.

John peddled harder. The man kept pace with him.

'When?' said the man.

'I don't know. What do you care?'

'I think you should. I think you should play.'

'I'll play it when I'm ready,' John replied, angrily. 'You leave me alone. You keep away from me, you hear? I don't want to play your stupid flute. I'll throw it away when I get in. I'll chuck it into a fire.'

'I'll haunt you until you do play.' The patience was gone, the threats poured forth. 'I'll jump into your dreams and drive you mad with fear. You can't get rid of me. I'll suffocate any peace you get. I'll cook your hopes and desires in an oven and eat them. You'll have no life, but I am there. Even after death, I shall be your eternal tormentor. Play the pipe, and end it now. Play the flute and I'll vanish.'

John then realised that he was talking with the creature who had been in his nightmares since he had arrived on the island.

He came to a skidding halt in front of the bungalow. Quickly looking round, he saw that he was alone again. The tattooed man had gone. What a weirdo! John didn't want to see him again, ever. He was shaking like a leaf in the wind. All he wanted to do was get rid of that flute. But would that be the answer? Perhaps if he did play it, the shadowman would indeed vanish forever?

He leaned his bike against the bungalow wall and went inside.

Mary was in his bedroom. She had been hanging clean shirts in John's wardrobe and had the flute in her hand. She was examining it closely.

'What's this, John?' she said, curiously, as he walked into the room. 'These markings – they look quite old.'

John was still trembling from his encounter, but he didn't want to worry his mother with more of his fears and concerns. She was too interested in the instrument to notice his pale complexion. Mary looked down the tube as he had done, holding it up to the ceiling light.

'There's something stuck down there.'

'Yes, I know.'

'Where did you say you got it?'

John said, 'I found it – in the forest. It was buried.'

'You must show me where you found it. Was there anything else there? Why did you dig in a particular place?'

'A – a man showed me.' John felt sick. He did not want to tell his mother any more than that. He was determined not to worry her any more than necessary. 'I met him walking in the rainforest. There was a green boulder, shaped like a shark, and the flute was in its mouth.'

Mary's lips tightened. 'You really ought not to go with strangers, John. I've told you about that.'

'I know,' he replied, miserably, 'but I was lost. He showed me the way back to the path.'

'Oh, it was that time you were lost in the middle of the island? You didn't mention this man before.'

John decided to let the misunderstandings go. 'It wasn't important. He showed me the path, that's all. I told you I met all these other people in there. The dancing people. You didn't seem to believe me about that, so why talk about another stranger? You thought I was out of my head, didn't you? Well, I wasn't.'

'Point taken.' She turned the dark-brown flute over in her hands. 'I'd like to do some tests on this, to see just how old it is. It looks as if the humus it was buried in has preserved it. I really would like to see this green shark of yours. Can you find it again?'

'Oh, yes. It's just below the Needle.'

Mary's head came up sharply. 'Really? How near?'

'In the valley, right underneath. If you stood by the Needle, you could spit on it.'

Mary smiled. 'Well, I'm not in the habit of spitting over cliffs, but this might be promising. You keep this for a while.' She handed him the flute. 'Look after it. I'm trusting you with it now, because I believe it to be a very rare artefact, something the museum would give its eye teeth for.'

'Museums don't have eye teeth, people do.'

She smiled again. 'Yes, of course. But listen, I'll have it tested, then if it is as ancient as it looks, I expect you'll want to donate it to the museum. It'll have your name underneath. "Discovered by Mr John Terangi." How does that sound? You'll probably get a finder's fee. That valley is public land, so there'll be no private owner to deal with. I can see we'll make an archaeologist out of you yet, young man.'

John flushed with pleasure at these words.

'Thanks, Mum.'

She left him alone in his bedroom, with the flute in his hand. He felt the smooth wood, ran his fingers over the carved characters. No doubt his mother would be able to decipher those markings, when she came to study it properly. Or perhaps they didn't mean anything at all, but were simply decorative, like many of the tattoos on the old people.

Tattoos.

He was reminded of the shadowman. Yes, he was still worried about the shadowman. Terrified in fact. But nothing had happened so far to harm him physically, so what was there to be scared about, except a lot of ghostly shapes in the night? There might be a lot of wailing and flitting and spectral dreams, but when it came down to it, nothing had actually hurt him, yet. Could the shadowman hurt him? He didn't think so, or the creature would have done so by now. Certainly he had been very angry, furious in fact, earlier in the evening. Why all the threats of haunting, if the shadowman could actually do something physical?

The shadowman had wanted John to play the flute. That had been the point of the threat. John studied the mouthpiece. It looked stained, perhaps with old spittle. It certainly did not look hygienic, as Sally had pointed out.

'Shall I soak this in bleach?' he called out to his mother.

Mary appeared in the doorway.

'Not if you value your life,' she said. 'You leave it as you found it. You can brush off any dirt, but if that *is* a valuable antique, you'll ruin it by soaking it in bleach, won't you?'

'Oh, yeah, didn't think of that.'

'Just leave it as it is, until I can get around to testing it. I've got a meeting tomorrow, with a few people, including a government minister, which I can't put off. The day after – that's Monday, isn't it? – you can stay off school – we'll go out to the site together and you can show me your greenstone shark. All right?'

'Sounds okay to me, Mum.'

'I thought the idea of a day's holiday might appeal to you. You'd better get washed for supper now. Then bed. Church first thing, then I've got to go off to my meeting. Can you find something to do with your friends, while I'm gone?'

'Sure.'

'I didn't think that would be a hardship.'

John went for his wash, then they had supper together on the veranda, where a cool wind blew in from the North, whipping up white veils of sprindrift along the reef. In New Zealand tubular surf often boomed along the beach, but here on Rarotonga it was only in stormy weather that the coral sands suffered any beatings from the waves. Mostly evenings were like this one, calm and gentle, with the sound of tender wavelets caressing white sand on which fiddler crabs had their hidey-holes. It was only out on the reef that the waves were tall.

Lying in bed, later, John knew that he would be visited. He steeled himself for the coming of the shadowman. When visitors came, however, they were in great number. They swarmed to his window with burnished bright eyes, their hands reaching for him.

12

The Opening of the Grave

John was dragged from his bed and forced through the open window. However, those who had come for him were friends, not enemies. It was the Tapairu. Up in the heavens was the biggest, most straw-coloured moon for many a long year and they had left the forest to dance on the golden sands for the first time in several centuries, risking the possibility of being seen by the many mortals who now lived on the island.

The beach was the natural place for the fairy revelry. In the past young fishermen had been caught up with the frolics of the Tapairu fairies and some of them had fallen in love with a beautiful sprite and had been lost from this world forever. There were stories of humans in fairyland who remained because they were enthralled.

As John was lifted by many hands, through the window, he managed to snatch up his flute. If there was to be music and dancing, he wanted to contribute. He had no idea how to play the instrument, but there was magic in fairyland and that would surely assist him in pulling the right notes from the long bamboo pipe.

Once through the window John skipped along with the Tapairu who, unlike Western fairies, were man-sized creatures. The fair hair set them apart from the mortals on the island, but essentially they were of Polynesian build and skin tone. Fairies on Rarotonga could fool – and often did – mortal watchers into believing they were humans.

John was caught up in the excitement which bubbled effervescently from the prancing group. Their restless feet danced even as they walked. They had rhythm in every muscle, timed movement in every bone. And there was great gaiety amongst them. There was joy like foam frothing up from the very ground upon which they walked. Even high up in the sky the clouds were golden suds, in which the moon bobbed like a huge round bar of soap.

'Where are we going?' cried John, his feet tripping along with the rest of them, the fairy in him coming out. 'Where's the dance?'

'On the shore,' cried a slim young maiden, skipping beside him. 'We shall dance amongst the scallop shells and seaweed tonight. We shall waken the crabs in their subterranean homes. We shall thrum the strand which slips into the sea and alarm the moray eels in their coral caves.'

There was a tiara of flowers around her brow, a garland of blooms around her neck. Her face was a heart-shaped delicate shell, with large eyes full of great wonder. Her words were like honey dripping from a busy hive. She skipped on, into the flock of fairies, her hair streaming out behind her, her slim arms and legs waving like weed in a current.

John had fallen in love with her the instant he had seen her.

Then he fell in love again, with the next maiden he saw, and the next, and the next, and found they were all around him and nothing to choose between one beautiful girl and those who flanked her. And the youthful-looking men were almost as beautiful as the women. They had the same sparkling eyes, the same lips that seemed to quiver and tremble with excitement, the same small curved noses that dilated with every small happy breath they took. Oh, they were handsome creatures.

Once the place on the beach, away from the houses, had been found the Tapairu began to dance in earnest. Their musicians now started to play. The flautists whipped forth thin reed pipes from their nestling places in their hair. The drummers rolled the drums from their backs. The conch-horn players brought their shell instruments to their lips and blew softly – crooning notes into the night air more mellow than the hoot of an owl, more melodic than the symphony of the sea.

John wanted to try his own flute.

He stopped and raised the instrument to his lips.

At last he was going to play!

Before the bamboo touched his mouth however, the fairy nearest John gave out a high shocking squeal. This creature sprang forward and dashed the pipe from his hands. The old tube of bamboo went spinning away from him, into the night, whirling a wind-song as it flew.

John cried, 'What did you do that for . . . ?' But the words were still half in his mouth when the flute struck a rock, end-on. Out of the pipe shot a dart which missed John's head by a few centimetres. The feather-fletched weapon struck a palm tree and buried its point deep into the bark. A fairy, nearest the leaning trunk, reached out and snapped the haft of the small spear, in order to get the scarlet feathers. These he handed to John, with a grave look, saying, 'A sorcerer's weapon!'

Another moment, and that dart would have buried its point in the back of John's throat.

'But how did you know?' cried John, staring at the flights in his hands.

'Why, from the symbols on the flute,' answered his

saviour. 'They are a magic incantation, a song-poem to attract fairies, a spell to entrance the nightdancers of Rarotonga.' The merry creature's eyes flashed like stars as he spoke. 'But any Tapairu seeing such markings would know where they came from. This is the booby trap of an evil wizard and a poor weak-minded one at that. A sorcerer who needs to kill a fairy to resurrect himself. But such a trap! A fairy child could see through it. We are amazed that you fell for this pathetic lure. There is more mortal in you than is good for any of our clan. You survived, but by luck, not by intelligence or magic or any of the respected fairy arts.'

John agreed, and asked if he might still be allowed to dance with them, even though he was unworthy to be in their presence.

They said he was just worthy enough.

The flute was forgotten. John pinned the scarlet feathers to his T-shirt. He knew from his mother's studies that in ancient Rarotonga red feathers were considered precious. In the olden days he would have been a wealthy person, even with such a small cluster of parrot's feathers.

The dancing went on all through the night. In the morning John fell exhausted to the sand. They carried him home and laid him in his bed. The flute they threw over the reef into the big wide Pacific Ocean. Who knew what sinister tunes would come out of a sorcerer's pipe? Perhaps a melody which would bring down trees? Or one that would wither the fruit on the vine? Or open the earth in great cracks? A bad wizard's instrument was not to be trusted. Let the barracuda play songs on it and the surprise be theirs!

When he woke in the morning, John's mind was clearer than it had been for months. His spirit felt refreshed and clean. At breakfast he told his mother he would take her straight to the green-stone shark. Mary took a team with her to the spot below the Needle. They lifted the great shark with winches and cables, to dig in the depression it left behind.

The first thing they came across were some small wooden images called *Ti'i* which magicians used to assist them in their spells.

'I think we've found it,' Mary said, excitedly. 'This is a sacred spot.'

'*Who* found it?' asked John.

She smiled at her son. 'You did, John. You did.'

Mary eventually came to the level of the grave. Stinking air hissed from the tomb as it was opened to reveal a grey skull with long black hair. Something foul and unholy seemed to waft from the orifices of the skull when it was uncovered, and one of Mary's helpers was concerned enough to fetch a priest. The priest, having been brought, sanctified the ground in and around the grave. When this was over the grave was opened wider, to reveal the whole of its contents.

Some rags. A dark anchor stake with a hole through its centre, once attached to the skull by a cord. A hank of dog's hair tied like a sheaf. A necklace of shark's teeth. The bones of a severed human hand bunched like a fist around a pumice stone.

'Look at that,' cried John, pointing at something grey and ugly which lay beside the skull. 'What's that?'

Mary took some tongs and lifted the artefact from the earth.

She had found her airo fai dagger, the terrible stingray's backbone with its thousands of small hooks.

'The sorcerer's weapon,' she said. 'An instrument of torture and painful death.'

'Is that what you're looking for, Mum?'

'This is it, John. I can't see the ritual spear though. I wonder what happened to that? There's always a taiaha spear in the grave.'

The artefacts having been removed from the tomb, the skull was covered over again, left to rest for all eternity.

On the way back to the bungalow with his triumphant parent, John asked, 'Where's the evil spirit of the sorcerer now, Mum?'

She looked at him quickly. 'What evil spirit?'

John felt that much of what he knew he should keep to himself.

'Well, when the sorcerer died, his spirit must have gone somewhere.'

'It's said the magician's kabu can live in anything belonging to him – any personal item which once belonged to him.'

'Oh, so it could be anywhere, really?'

'Yes – if we believed in such things.'

Before John left for New Zealand, a month later, he gave Mati and Sally a scarlet feather each.

'Just something to remember me by,' he said.

Mati looked at the feather dubiously.

'They used to be like diamonds to the old Polynesians,' John explained, noticing his friend's expression. 'And that feather once belonged to a wizard.'

'Really?' said Mati, looking at it differently. 'In that case I'll pin it on my Manchester United shirt!'

'Soccer,' sniffed Sally. '*I'm* going to put mine in a glass vial and seal it, so that it stays as red forever.'

'How romantic,' sniffed Mati.

On the flight back to Auckland, John was very quiet, and his mother *thought* she understood. He had explained to her that he had lost the ancient flute on the beach. She thought he was feeling upset by that. At the airport they hired a car and drove towards their house. The boxes of artefacts had gone on to the museum. Already there was a glass case in a prominent position ready for the airo fai. Like Sally's vial, it would be sealed.

Over a green hill, around a bend on which some

ribbonwood trees stood in stately stances, and on towards the house.

Much as he had loved Rarotonga, the home of his ancestors, John felt a sense of relief.

He was safe home.

There were many visitors to the museum in the following years, curious to see the sorcerer's dagger. Most stared at it with revulsion, wondering at the depths to which some men could sink. Others, professors and students of ancient history, studied it with interest. Still others wondered what the fuss was all about, since as fishermen they caught stingrays and saw such bones when their catch was cut open. It was a curio which brought Mary Terangi a little fame in her small circle of archaeologists, and she too often went to view her find.

None however, including Mary, came away from the viewing without a sense of dread in their hearts. Staring at the ugly dagger, that wizard's ritual sacrificial stabbing weapon, brought on an eerie feeling of being watched by some nefarious entity, some wicked presence. Uncomfortable, visitors would turn and stare around them, at masks on the walls, or wood and stone carvings, wondering if that feeling were being generated by some other item in the room.

If they were alone, they left the museum quickly.

If with others, they made excuses, and moved on.

Not long after a year had passed, Mary discovered a whole batch of Samoan war clubs at a dig on one of the islands. The airo fai made way for an exhibition of this wonderful find. The dagger in its glass container went into the archives of the museum. It stood on some dusty shelf, high up out of reach, and to certain knowledge is still there today.